the loft

THE MEMORY HOUSE SERIES, BOOK TWO

BETTE LEE CROSBY

THE LOFT
The Memory House Series, Book Two

Copyright © 2015 by Bette Lee Crosby

Cover design: damonza.com
Formatting by Author E.M.S.
Editor: Ekta Garg

This is a work of fiction. While, as in all fiction, the literary perceptions and insights are based on life experiences and conclusions drawn from research, all names, characters, places and specific instances are products of the author's imagination and used fictitiously. No actual reference to any real person, living or dead, is intended or inferred.

ISBN-13: 978-0-9960803-8-5

BENT PINE PUBLISHING
Port Saint Lucie, FL

Published in the United States of America

OTHER BOOKS BY THIS AUTHOR

*"There are only two ways to live your life.
One is as though nothing is a miracle.
The other is as though everything is a miracle."*

~ Albert Einstein ~

THE FIRST STONE

They say that somewhere far beyond what mortals see there is a scale of life, and for each moment of happiness a stone of sorrow is dropped onto the scale.

When the Keeper of the Scale saw that Annie Cross's life had been weighted with sorrow for far too long, he selected a stone the color of an early morning sunrise. It was round, worn smooth and without jagged edges. He gave a smile of satisfaction, then dropped the stone onto the happiness side of Annie's scale. That was the day she knocked on Judge Oliver Doyle's door.

As she looked into the blue of his eyes, she knew he was the one.

EXACTLY 3.2 MILES FROM OPHELIA Browne's Memory House Bed and Breakfast there is a small clapboard church. It is set back from the street and surrounded by oaks that have stood for centuries. If you lift your head and search the treetops, you will find the steeple. The tip of it is just a bit above the tallest oak, and when the sun is high in the sky a person must shade their eyes to catch

even a glimpse. Although the steeple is sometimes difficult to see, on Sunday morning when the bells chime they can be heard throughout all of Burnsville.

Pastor Willoughby claims the Good Shepherd Church will accommodate 90 parishioners, but today 120 people have crowded in. It is the first Saturday of June yet hot as the middle of August. The side windows have been thrown open and a soft breeze drifts across the room, but it is not enough to cool the crowd squeezed shoulder to shoulder.

The first time Ophelia came to this church was the year she and Edward were married. That was almost seventy years ago, yet nothing has changed. When she steps into the vestibule her mind slides back to a sadder day, the day of Edward's funeral. Before the melancholy of remembering can take hold, a young man steps up to her.

"May I?" he asks and offers his arm.

Ophelia smiles. "Thank you," she says and slides her hand into the opening that is offered.

Charlie Doyle is Oliver's brother. Together he and Ophelia walk slowly down the aisle.

The first pew is the only spot where there are still seats. The left side is reserved for the bride's family, the right side for the groom's. Charlie guides Ophelia to the pew on the left side and waits for her to smooth her skirt and sit. Once she is seated, he gives a pleasant nod and turns back to the vestibule. Ophelia is the only person in that pew. She is Annie's family.

The tall white-haired man on the right side looks across at Ophelia and smiles. He stands, goes to her and extends his hand.

"Please," he says, "come and sit with Laura and me. We should be one family now."

Ophelia takes his hand and stands. "Thank you, Ethan." They have met only once before, but Ophelia feels she has known him for a long time. His eyes are the same blue as Oliver's, and

2

although his lips are thinner now his smile is the same. Ethan Allen Doyle is Oliver's daddy.

MOMENTS AFTER OPHELIA IS SEATED, Oliver and Charlie walk down the aisle and stand side by side to the left of the altar. The organ then fills the room with the sound of music, and everyone stands.

Giselle is first down the aisle; she works with Annie at the library and is the matron of honor. When she reaches the altar, she steps to the right.

The organist then stomps on the pedals and starts to play the traditional wedding march. All heads turn.

Annie appears in the doorway. Her veil is pushed back from her face, and she carries a bouquet of the bright pink peonies grown in Ophelia's garden. She smiles and starts down the aisle. She has dreamed of this moment for more years than she has known Oliver. It is just as she imagined, yet it is different.

Michael Stavros is not the man waiting at the end of the aisle; it is Oliver. And she is no longer a girl blinded by the thought of love. Annie is now a woman, a woman who has learned to love and be loved. It is the kind of love that runs deep and is destined to last forever. The night Oliver slipped an engagement ring on her finger, she could see the future as easily as she sees the past.

Today they will start to create their own memories, memories that Annie hopes will one day be found in the objects they leave behind.

OLIVER REACHES OUT AND TAKES her hand; together they turn to Pastor Willoughby.

He starts to speak. "Today we are gathered together..."

3

Annie and Oliver have both written their own vows. In hers she promises to love him always and unconditionally.

"I will forever be your best friend and stand beside you," she says, "for as long as the stars shine in the night sky and, God willing, even longer." The words are soft and gentle as she speaks them.

A tear falls from Ophelia's eye as she listens. She can remember making just such a promise to Edward, but long after he was gone the stars still lit the sky and she could do nothing but ache for his body to again lie beside hers.

Oliver tells Annie she has brought a newfound happiness to his life, that the ordinary things of yesterday are no longer ordinary but amazing because he can see them through her eyes.

"Although I may be an imperfect being," he says, "I will for the rest of my days love you, honor you and cherish you with every ounce of my heart and soul."

They exchange rings, and as they share a kiss the organist begins Beethoven's *Ode to Joy*. She plays softly at first, but when Annie and Oliver turn to the congregation the music grows louder and the church bells begin to chime as they do on Sunday morning.

Oliver whispers, "I love you, Annie Doyle," and they start back down the aisle together.

ANNIE

It may seem like this special day is the beginning of my story, but it's not. My story began a year ago when I knocked on Ophelia Browne's door. Back then I thought she was just a sweet little old lady with a bed and breakfast and a magical potpourri that smells like whatever you're thinking of. It may be difficult to imagine such a potpourri, but that's only because you don't know Ophelia. She's a woman who can find the magic hidden in everyday things.

When she first told me it was possible to connect to a memory someone had left behind in a forgotten object, I thought she was joking. But once I experienced it for myself, I knew it was true. I guess if you want to live life to the fullest, you've got to be open-minded about the things that seem unbelievable.

OPHELIA TAUGHT ME HOW TO touch an object and find the memory in it. At first I thought maybe it was her dandelion tea that enabled me to do this, but she said it was more than likely something I was born with. She claims this ability is a gift given only to those with sensitive souls. I can't say whether or not this is true, but I can say I'm very glad for having met Ophelia. Knowing her has changed my life.

It began the day she showed me the bicycle in the storage shed. The minute I touched it, I heard a boy's laughter. The sound of his laughter so intrigued me that I wanted to know more about him.

The thing is, you can't just pull a memory out of something the way you'd pull a splinter from your finger. It takes time and lots of love.

For months I worked on that bicycle, polishing it, shining it and always listening for another word or two from the boy. Little by little it came to me. I felt his heartbeat, and I knew of his fear, but I never knew his name. Then one day I found a book called The Wisdom of Judicial Judgment in the Practice of Law. *The minute my hand touched that book, I knew the author, Ethan Allen Doyle, was my bicycle boy. Yes, he's Oliver's daddy, but he's also my bicycle boy.*

My search for Ethan Allen is what led me to knock on Oliver's door.

YOU CAN TELL ME SEVEN *ways from Sunday there's no such thing as magic, and you might be right. But since I've allowed my heart to believe in the things Ophelia taught me, my life is filled with the magic of love and happiness.*

And that's something there is no question about.

THE SWANS

The reception is held in the side yard of Memory House. It is what Annie asked for, and Oliver has arranged everything. The caterers arrived at the break of dawn, and by the time the guests come from the church there are several white tents dotting the lawn and a bubbling champagne fountain in the center.

Three days ago a pair of trumpeter swans came from out of nowhere and settled on the pond. They are long-necked and graceful. Annie believes it is a good omen. Like Ophelia, she has come to believe in such signs.

She whispers in Oliver's ear, "I think this means we'll be mated for life."

Oliver laughs. "I know we'll be mated for life and not because of the swans."

Annie stretches up and kisses his cheek. His practicality is one of the many things she loves about Oliver. Even though she has told him the story of the bicycle boy and how she came to be standing on his doorstep that night, he still believes it was simply a stroke of good fortune that brought her to him.

When Annie spots Ophelia sitting in one of the wicker chairs placed about the yard, she makes her way through the crowd and squats beside her.

"Without you none of this would have happened," she says. "How can I possibly thank you?"

Ophelia leans forward and lovingly traces her hand along Annie's cheek. "You don't need to thank me. Just having you with me for this past year is more than I could have asked for."

"Well, don't think you're rid of me," Annie says with a grin. "I plan on working in the apothecary two days a week and coming over weekends to help with the garden."

Ophelia sets her tea aside and takes Annie's hand in hers. "You'll do nothing of the sort," she says. "I'll be just fine. What I want you to do is to go off on your honeymoon and have the most wonderful time of your life."

Annie laughs. "That shouldn't be too hard."

THE PARTY LASTS UNTIL THE sky settles into dusk. When the crowd thins, Ethan Allen spies Ophelia sitting alone and walks over. He is carrying two glasses of champagne.

"I thought you could use this," he says.

He hands the glass to Ophelia and sits beside her.

It has been a long day; happy, yes, but also emotionally draining for Ophelia. She accepts the glass and is glad to have it. "Thank you," she says and smiles.

They sit in silence for a minute; then Ethan says, "I'm glad Oliver has Annie." He turns to Ophelia and adds, "It's not good for anyone to be alone."

Ophelia looks down at the hand not holding the champagne. She still wears the narrow gold band Edward once placed on her finger.

"That surely is true," she says sadly.

"So what are you going to do?" he asks.

Ethan grins, and the years fall away. Ophelia sees the face of Annie's bicycle boy. For a moment she is held spellbound; then she shakes the image loose.

"Do about what?" she asks.

"About staying here alone," he says.

"I'm not alone," she replies indignantly.

He leans forward and rests his hand on the arm of her chair. "With Annie moving into Wyattsville, you will be," he says.

"I will not!" she snaps back. "I have friends. Customers too. There's not a day that passes when I don't have a dozen or more people stop by the apothecary."

Ethan smiles at Ophelia's feistiness. She is a reminder of the eleven-year-old boy who made his way to Wyattsville. He can almost hear himself saying *I don't need nothing from nobody!* It's what you say when your back is to the wall and you've got no place else to go.

"Why, with taking care of customers and tending my garden," Ophelia continues, "I'm busy morning 'til night."

"Well, then, maybe you need a housekeeper."

Ophelia's eyes grow wide and she gasps. "Housekeeper?" Before he has a chance to say anything more, she charges ahead. "Why? Do you think my house is dirty? Are the beds unmade? Is the floor not swept?"

"I only meant—"

"I don't care a fig for what you meant," she snaps. "I've run this bed and breakfast all by myself for over fifty years, and I can run it for fifty more if I've a mind to!"

"I don't doubt that," Ethan says, "but Laura and I live in a lovely retirement village in Florida, and we thought maybe—"

"I'm not retired!"

Ignoring her comment, Ethan continues. "In our complex we've got a gardening club that would be delighted to have an expert like you teach them—"

"I told you, I'm not retired!"

Ethan chuckles. "So you said. But if you ever should decide to retire, I want you to know we'd welcome the opportunity to have you."

The muscles in Ophelia's face relax. "That's very nice of you," she says politely. She swallows the last of her champagne then adds, "I'll keep it in mind if I ever do decide to retire."

Ethan stands, but before he turns away he bends down and kisses Ophelia's cheek. "You remind me of Grandma Olivia," he whispers, "and she was one damn fine woman."

AFTER EVERYONE IS GONE, THE waiters start to clean up. Glasses and dishes are put into plastic bins and loaded into the truck parked in the driveway. Tablecloths disappear into a laundry bag, and the tables themselves are folded flat and carted off. Tomorrow another crew will come and take the tents. Then it will be as it was before, and the party will exist only in Ophelia's memory.

How sad, she thinks, *that the most wonderful things disappear so quickly and yet sorrow hangs on forever.*

ETHAN ALLEN DOYLE

You might think it strange that I suggested Ophelia come to Florida, especially since we haven't known each other for that long. But I've been in her shoes, so I know how it feels to be alone and without a soul to turn to. The last thing in the world you'll do is ask for help. You build a defensive barrier around yourself, and you're afraid that one moment of weakness will bring that wall crashing down.

I see a lot of myself in Ophelia. I was eleven when Grandma Olivia took me in, and I shudder to think what would have happened if she hadn't. My mama and daddy were both dead, and I didn't have anybody else to turn to. Olivia Doyle wasn't even my real grandma. She'd simply married a granddaddy I'd never even laid eyes on, and he was already dead when I got there.

I was sassy-mouthed, cussed like a sailor and had the man who killed my daddy looking for me, but Grandma Olivia overlooked all of that. She said we were family and family had to stick together. If she could find room in her heart to love a kid like that, Laura and I can certainly make room in our lives for one sweet little old lady.

Ophelia is ninety, but she doesn't seem it. She's sharp as a tack and plenty spry. Unfortunately she's as sassy and independent as I was, so

I'm sure that when she makes up her mind to do something there's nobody who's going to change it.

I know Annie will keep a close eye on Ophelia. Oliver will too.

I told him the same thing I'm telling you and he said, "Don't worry, Dad, I'll see she's well taken care of."

He will. I'm certain of it. Oliver's serious-minded and carries responsibilities like a briefcase shackled to his arm.

I'm mighty proud to have a boy like him, and I think if Grandma Olivia were here to see him she'd be just as proud.

The Dream

When the caterer's truck finally leaves, Memory House is silent except for an occasional squawk from the ducks on the pond. Ophelia climbs the stairs to the loft where she sleeps. It will be comforting to lie in bed and search the night sky for a few familiar friends.

She changes into a soft cotton nightgown, plumps the pillow and crawls into bed. Above her there is a large skylight—the skylight Edward built. On nights when she is most lonely, she can look up and imagine him there among the stars he loved so dearly.

Tonight they shine brighter than usual. She can see the constellation of Pegasus clearly. She searches her mind for the names of the stars in the constellation but can remember only one: Enif. It shines more brightly than any of the others.

Even after Ophelia has closed her eyes she can still see the night sky, and she can remember the sound of Edward's voice naming each individual star.

"BEAUTIFUL, ISN'T IT?" A VOICE SAYS.

It comes from behind her, but Ophelia knows without turning that it is Edward.

"Yes, it is," she answers. She feels the warmth of his hands on her shoulders.

"We had some good years, didn't we, Opie?"

Ophelia feels herself smile. Opie. It is a name only he uses, and it is good to hear it again. Then she sighs. "It's been so long."

"Too long."

"It hasn't been easy," she says, "taking care of this house, the garden, the apothecary…"

"I know." He gives her shoulder an affectionate squeeze. "I was glad when the girl came. It was good to see you laugh again."

"She's gone now," Ophelia says sadly.

"I know."

She feels the tug of his arm as he pulls her closer to his chest.

"Maybe you too should leave here," he says. "Find a place where there's less work and someone to watch over you."

"I could never," she says. "This is where I belong."

"It's not good for a person to be alone," he says.

"I'm not alone. You're here with me." She snuggles deeper into his arms. "I stay here because this is where I can look into the night sky and find you."

He laughs. It is the same gentle laugh she has heard a thousand times before.

For a moment there is only silence and the joy of having him hold her. She would like to remain like this forever, but soon he will disappear just as he always does.

He knows her thoughts, and again there is the soft sound of his laughter. "Opie, my dear sweet Opie. I don't live here in this house. I'm alive inside your heart. I'll go wherever you go."

"But here in this room—"

"Look at the sky," he says. "On nights when there's a cloud

cover overhead, you can't see the stars but you know they're still there."

Ophelia smiles, realizing this is true.

"So am I," he says. "No matter where you are, I am with you and I will be until the end of days."

She gives a melancholy sigh. "But I miss you terribly."

He touches the side of his face to hers, and she can feel the heat of his breath.

"I know," he answers. "In time we will be together again."

"When?"

Ophelia feels the movement of his body as he shrugs.

"It's still in the future," he says. "I don't know when it will happen, but on that day I'll come for you."

"You're here now. Why can't you just take me with you?" She turns to face him and is startled. Never before has she seen Edward older than he was the day he died, but now he has white hair and looks remarkably like Ethan Allen Doyle.

"Edward?" she says, but before there is time for an answer he is gone.

OPHELIA BOLTS UP AND SCREAMS out his name, but it is too late. Now there is only the empty room and the rose of a new dawn drifting across the skylight. She is still groggy from sleep and wants to hold onto the dream, but it is impossible. She remembers only that he was there and knows only that he is now gone.

She sobs and lowers her head into her lap. "Oh, Edward."

TODAY IS SUNDAY, A DAY when almost no one comes to the apothecary. It stretches in front of her like a long road to travel. Ophelia climbs from the bed with the steely resolve that has carried her through the years.

For breakfast she makes blueberry pancakes. It is the same breakfast she sets out for guests, but today they seem tasteless. She sprinkles a heaping tablespoon of brown sugar on the pancakes, but they still are flavorless as cardboard. Finally, she scrapes them into the garbage can. She was not all that hungry anyway, she tells herself. Instead she will brew a full pot of dandelion tea, perhaps with a bit of chamomile and a sprig of mint. Then she will sit on the back porch and read or perhaps crochet.

After the kitchen is cleaned and the breakfast dishes put away, Ophelia pulls a book of Walt Whitman poems from the shelf. She is just about to settle on the porch when she hears the sound of the Good Shepherd's bells. They are calling people to worship.

The memory of yesterday is fresh in her mind. It has a certain warmth in it. People she has known for years go there. Friends shake hands and hug one another. The thought of a casual embrace or her hand touching another is welcomed on a day such as this. She sets the book aside and takes a lightweight jacket from the hall closet. Being at the Good Shepherd Church is far better than being alone.

Some days Ophelia can tolerate the loneliness, but today it is harder. Why, she cannot say. Perhaps because she has grown used to Annie being there, or maybe because of the dream. Feeling Edward's closeness and then having him disappear again freshens the pain of his absence.

Ophelia has not driven for well over a year, but she has not forgotten how. It is like walking; you take a single step then it all comes back. Anyway, it is just over three miles to the church. Not a busy road. An easy drive. Nothing to be nervous about.

"Don't carry on like a helpless twit," she tells herself and takes the car key from the basket in the kitchen.

When she slides into the driver's seat Ophelia feels her heart pounding against her chest. "Silly old woman," she grumbles and turns the key in the ignition.

The engine sputters and coughs then dies. She tries again. There is a momentary growl of resistance; then it surges to life. She adjusts the rear view mirror and backs out.

Ophelia is halfway to the church when the first pain hits. It is like a hammer slamming against her back and pummeling her ribcage. She slows the car, but before she can pull to the side of the road the second one comes. It is worse than the first. She falls across the steering wheel, and the car slowly rolls over the edge of the road. When it finally comes to a stop, the right wheel is in the creek that runs alongside the road.

SHORT HONEYMOON

On Sunday morning Oliver is up and dressed before Annie even opens one eye. They will honeymoon in New York, and he has the week planned: several Broadway shows, dining in five star restaurants and strolling through Central Park. He bends down and kisses her nose.

"Wake up, sleepyhead," he says. "We've got to get going."

She sits up and rubs her eyes. "What time is it?"

"Almost seven," he says and sets a cup of coffee on the nightstand beside her.

Annie pushes the covers back and climbs out of bed. "Isn't there any tea?"

"No," he says. "Sorry. I got so involved with the reception I forgot to get it."

A year ago Annie couldn't start the day without a tall mug of coffee; now she dislikes the bitter taste. She wrinkles her nose.

"I'd like to check on Ophelia anyway," she says. "Let's stop by the house, and I can grab a cup there."

Oliver winces. "I'd like to be on the road by eight," he replies. "It's a seven-hour drive, and we've got early dinner reservations."

This evening is meant to be a surprise so he doesn't mention that the reservation is at One if by Land, Two if by Sea, a quaint carriage house restaurant in the West Village. It's a place where reservations usually require a six-month wait. He wants this night to be special and has asked for a table in the corner with a bottle of champagne and a ribboned rose for Annie.

"Would you settle for a chai from Starbucks?" he asks.

She smiles. "I suppose so," she says and heads for the shower.

THEY ARE ABOUT TO TURN onto Route 95 when Annie pulls her cell phone out of her purse and punches in Ophelia's number. It rings a dozen or more times, but there is no answer.

"That's strange," she says. "Where would Ophelia be this early in the morning?"

"Outside in the garden?" Oliver suggests.

"It's only nine-fifteen."

"Perhaps she went to the store? Or church?"

Annie frowns. "I certainly hope not. She doesn't drive anymore."

"Maybe one of the neighbors came and picked her up."

She shakes her head. "I don't think so. Something about this doesn't feel right…"

Annie hits redial and waits. Still there is no answer. She sits her purse back on the floor but holds the phone in her hand.

After she has tried several times, Oliver suggests calling a neighbor.

Annie gives an absent nod. "Emma Landon lives just down the road. I'll call and ask her to check on Ophelia."

Annie taps Search and types "white pages directory-Burnsville, VA" then puts in Emma Landon's name.

The phone reports there is no listing.

She types in George Landon.

Still no listing.

She tries Bertha Warren and finally meets with success.

After punching in Bertha's number she waits. It rings sixteen, maybe seventeen times, but there is no answer.

The ridges across Annie's forehead deepen. "This really is strange."

Oliver pulls to the side of the road. "I'll call Andrew and ask him to go over and make sure she's okay." Andrew Steen was Oliver's law partner and is still his friend.

"It's a forty-minute drive from his house," Annie says. "Do you think he'll mind doing it?"

Oliver shakes his head. He is already dialing the number.

Andrew answers on the first ring, and Oliver explains the problem.

"It's the white house on Haber Street," he says. "All the way at the end." He rattles off Annie's cell phone number and tells Andrew to call as soon as he gets there.

As they pull back onto Route 95, Annie says, "I'm concerned." The truth is she is worried, but she uses the word concerned.

Oliver glances over. He sees her lips stretched tight and a line of furrows hovering above her brow.

"Want me to turn around?" he asks.

Annie would like to go back; she would like to know Ophelia is okay and nothing is wrong. But this is their honeymoon. Oliver has special plans, and she doesn't want to disappoint him.

"No," she answers. "Not yet."

Her finger nervously picks at the edge of her cell phone case and he hears the apprehension in her voice. "Are you sure?"

"Pretty sure," she says. "Hopefully it won't be long before Andrew calls."

Oliver slows the car and eases off at the next exit. He crosses under the overpass and pulls onto Route 95 Southbound.

"Thank you," Annie says softly. A few moments pass before she speaks again. "I'm sorry. I know this isn't how you planned to start our honeymoon."

Oliver stretches his arm across the seat and lifts her hand into his. "There's nothing to be sorry about," he says. "Our honeymoon is only one week. We've still got a lifetime of love to look forward to."

"True, but—"

"There are no buts," Oliver cuts in. "Even if I could, I wouldn't change a thing about you. The kind of love you have for Ophelia is a rare and unselfish thing." He glances over and smiles. "I'm hoping that one day you'll love me as much as you love her."

A tear rolls down Annie's cheek. She brushes it back and looks across at Oliver. He doesn't have the chiseled chin and dark eyes of Michael Stavros, but to her he is the most beautiful man in the world.

"I already do love you that much," she says.

He slows the car and eases onto the shoulder of the road. Unbuckling his seat belt, he reaches across the console and pulls Annie into an embrace.

"Annie Doyle," he says, "I love you more than I ever dreamed possible."

He presses his mouth to hers, and it is so much more than just a kiss. It is his promise of a lifetime.

When their lips part and he moves back behind the steering wheel, Annie gives a deep sigh. She knows he is her Edward; he is the whole of her life.

"We'll have tomorrow and all the tomorrows after that," he says. "But for now we have to go back and make sure Ophelia is okay."

They are crossing into Virginia when Annie's cell phone rings. The caller ID tells her it is Andrew Steen.

"Are you at the house yet?" she asks.

"Yes," Andrew answers, "but there's no one here."

"Sometimes she's slow answering," Annie says. "Did you ring the cowbell over by the apothecary?"

"Yes. And I checked the garden and backyard. She's not here."

"Is the car in the garage?"

"I don't know," Andrew says. "There's no window."

"Go around back," Annie tells him. "That door is never locked."

"Hold on."

Annie listens to the sound of footsteps and the squeak of the rusty hinge.

After a few moments Andrew is back on the line. "There's no car in the garage."

"Is there any sign of trouble? A broken window? Trampled bushes?"

"Not that I can see," Andrew answers.

Annie lets out a whoosh of air that is drawn from the pit of her stomach. "Oh, dear…"

Oliver is going seventy-eight miles per hour; he pushes down on the pedal and takes it up to eighty-five.

"We'll be there in forty minutes or less," he says.

"Do you want me to do anything else?" Andrew asks.

"I guess not," Annie replies. She wants to believe there is a logical reason why the car is gone, but right now she cannot think of one. Her only thought is that Ophelia is behind the wheel of the car.

AFTER ANDREW HANGS UP, THEY ride in silence for almost a minute. Oliver wants to say something that will ease Annie's mind, but he knows words are useless at a time like this.

"Perhaps Ophelia drove to church," he finally offers. "There's almost no traffic on Creekside road, so she should be fine."

"She hasn't driven in over a year. Maybe longer."

"But that doesn't mean she can't."

"I hope that's true," Annie says. By now she has picked the plastic loose from one whole corner of her cell phone case.

ANNIE CROSS...NOW DOYLE

I'll never forgive myself if something has happened to Ophelia.

I should have known better than to go off and leave her alone. She's ninety years old. A woman her age shouldn't have to fend for herself. Someone should be there to drive her wherever she wants to go or call for help if she gets sick.

It's easy to forget she's getting on in years because she doesn't act old, but that's a poor excuse for me being so thoughtless. I should have ignored her objections and made arrangements for someone to stay with her.

I don't say this to Oliver, but I know Ophelia gets nervous in the car, even when she's sitting in the passenger seat. Sometimes if I turn a corner a bit too fast, she'll grab onto the armrest so tightly her knuckles go white. That's not the kind of person who should be driving.

I want to believe this is all just some crazy mix-up; that maybe George Landon borrowed the car to drive Ophelia and Emma to church or the vegetable market; but there's a gnawing fear inside my heart saying that's not the case. The truth is I'm scared to death she's in trouble.

Don't ask me what kind of trouble or how I know, because I don't have an answer. I can only tell you what I feel.

Right now, I'm praying Ophelia is safe. If we get home and find she's okay, I swear I'll never again go off and leave her alone like this.

Never. Not under any circumstances.

THE CALL

Annie is still holding the phone in her hand when it rings again. The caller ID reads Walter Bassinger. The name is familiar, but at the moment she doesn't recall from where.

"Annie Cross?" he asks.

"Yes," she answers.

"I don't know if you remember me," he says. "We met at the Memory House Apothecary. You mixed up some ginger root tea for Louise…"

"Yes, I remember." Already Annie senses something is wrong. "Is this about Ophelia?"

"I'm afraid so," he answers. "There was an accident on Creekside Road."

The words ricochet through Annie's head. What she feared most has come to pass. Although the thought is almost too painful to consider, she somehow summons enough courage.

"Is Ophelia okay?" she asks.

"I don't know," Walter replies. "When I found her she was slumped over the steering wheel. I called for an ambulance, and they took her to Mercy."

Tears already overflow Annie's eyes. "Thank you," she says with a sniffle. "Was she conscious? Did she say anything?"

"No. She was still passed out when they took her away."

"How did you know who to…"

"Your telephone number was in her purse."

Annie asks a few more questions, but there are no answers. By the time the call ends, her hands are trembling. She turns to Oliver and says, "Ophelia's at Mercy Hospital."

He cuts across the line of traffic and makes a sharp turn onto Begonia Boulevard.

"We'll be there in less than ten minutes," he says.

WHEN THEY ARRIVE AT THE hospital, Oliver pulls up to the emergency entrance.

"Go ahead," he says. "I'll park the car and be right behind you."

Annie pushes through the double doors, hurries to the desk and asks for Ophelia Browne.

A young nurse with the expression of someone whose feet hurt glances up. "What name?" she asks.

"Ophelia Browne. She was in an automobile accident. An elderly woman, silver hair, slender—"

"Are you family?" the nurse asks.

Annie nods. "Yes. I'm her…" She hesitates for a moment as she decides whether to be the granddaughter or daughter.

"Granddaughter," she finally says. "Can you tell me how she's doing?"

"They've taken her to the O-R. Have a seat and the doctor will be down to talk to you when the procedure is over."

"But can't anyone tell me anything now?"

"Have a seat," the nurse repeats. "We'll let you know as soon as we have something."

When Oliver comes in, he scans the room. He spies Annie sitting in the waiting area and joins her.

"Have they told you anything yet?" he asks.

She shakes her head.

ANNIE AND OLIVER SPEND THE FIRST day of their honeymoon sitting side by side in the waiting room. It is filled with little snippets of tragedy: a boy with an arm that appears broken, a young mother trying to comfort a crying baby, a fearful-looking old man clutching a woman's purse to his chest.

As the hours drag on, Annie's hope grows thinner. She drops her head onto Oliver's shoulder and cries. He wraps his arm around her and tries to find the right words. There are none.

IT IS ALMOST SIX O'CLOCK before the doctor comes to the waiting room. He introduces himself as Alex Milburn and says Ophelia is stable now.

"Your grandmother had a massive heart attack," he tells Annie. "She's lucky to be alive."

"Will she be okay?" Oliver asks.

Doctor Milburn gives a solemn shrug. "Because of her age there's no guarantee. The next twenty-four hours will be crucial." He adds that Ophelia is now being moved to the Coronary Care Unit where skilled nurses will watch her every breath.

Annie's knees go weak as she grabs hold of Oliver's arm. "Is there anything we can do?"

"Pray," he answers. "If there is no further damage and she makes it through the night, her chances of recovery are fairly good. But the probability is she'll need therapy and ongoing care."

"Whatever it costs," Oliver says. "Just do what you have to do."

The silver-haired doctor gives an understanding nod. "It's not a question of money. She's already getting the best possible care." He says the angioplasty went well, and it appears the blockage has been cleared. His words end there. He speaks only of what is, not what will be.

AFTER OPHELIA IS SETTLED IN the CCU, Annie is permitted a short visit.

"Ten minutes," a stern-faced nurse says. "The patient needs her rest."

Annie hates to hear Ophelia called "the patient." She is so much more.

When she enters the room Ophelia's eyes are open, but she looks dazed. She has the look of a woman who remembers nothing. Annie leans over the bed and kisses her wrinkled cheek.

"You gave us quite a scare," she says.

Ophelia offers a weak smile. "Sorry," she mumbles.

"The doctor said you're going to be just fine," Annie lies. "But you've got to get lots of rest and take it easy for a while."

"Okay." Ophelia closes her eyes.

For the remainder of the allotted ten minutes Annie stands beside the bed holding Ophelia's hand in hers. "It's going to be all right," she repeats over and over, but beneath the bravado of those words there is the sound of a frightened little girl.

After what seems like only moments the nurse comes into the room, gives Annie a nod and taps the face of her watch. She turns and leaves without speaking.

Annie leans down and kisses Ophelia again.

"I have to go now," she says in a low voice, "but I'll be back tomorrow morning." She stands, starts toward the door then reverses herself and turns back.

Leaning over the bed with her mouth next to Ophelia's ear she whispers, "I love you, Ophelia. I love you just as much as Edward did. Please don't leave me."

Ophelia's eyes are closed, and she appears to be sleeping.

Annie doesn't know whether Ophelia has heard what she said. She crosses the cavernous outer room and steps into the hallway where Oliver is waiting. There she gives way to a flood of tears.

Oliver feels the tremble of her shoulders as she sobs into his chest.

"Don't cry, sweetheart." He places his hand in the hollow of her back and gently massages it.

"It's going to be okay," he says softly. "Ophelia's getting the best of care, and she's strong. By tomorrow she'll probably be sitting up and asking to go home."

He lies to Annie just as she has lied to Ophelia. It is what you do to comfort the fears of someone you love.

THAT NIGHT THEY DO NOT return to Wyattsville. Instead they go to Memory House and stay in Annie's old room. Here they are closer to the hospital, and they plan to come back early.

Although she has done little but sit and wait, Annie is tired to the bone. It is an exhaustion borne of sorrow, an exhaustion not appeased by rest. Sleep is impossible to come by, so she brews a pot of dandelion tea and moves to the screened back porch. Dandelion tea is usually sweet but this tea is not; it is filled with the bitterness of her tears.

OLIVER DOYLE

I t's not two full days since we stood in front of the pastor and I swore I'd protect Annie for the rest of her life. Now here I am, helpless as a baby. I see her pain and feel it in my own heart, but all I can do is hold her in my arms and wipe her tears.

I promise her things that are not in my power to give. Ophelia is going to make it, I say, but only God knows if that's the truth.

Last night we sat on the back porch for a long time, and Annie talked about the things she and Ophelia had shared. She drank four mugs of dandelion tea claiming it would help her sleep. It didn't. She was up most of the night. She tried to be quiet, but I heard her moving around.

Near dawn I heard the door to the apothecary click open. Because I was worried about her, I got up and went to check. She was behind the counter mulling a dish of crushed leaves. Supposedly it was a healing tea she was going to brew for Ophelia.

Annie believes in that stuff; I don't. I was tempted to say the doctors are already giving her the medication she needs but thought better of it and kept my doubts to myself. I figure if Annie really believes in these things, who am I to argue?

I asked if this was like the dandelion tea she drinks, but she shook her head.

"No, this one has evening primrose, astragalus root, and hawthorn," she said. "Ophelia says it brings back a person's good memories and heals their heart."

Even though I doubted any tea could do such a thing, I was glad it made Annie feel like she's doing something to help. Let me tell you, that's a lot better than sitting around feeling as helpless as I am.

HEALING TEA

On Monday morning Annie is back at Mercy Hospital at 7:45. Oliver comes with her, and he carries a bouquet of hyacinth clipped from Ophelia's garden.

The duty nurse looks up and shakes her head. "Sorry, no flowers, and only one visitor at a time."

"You go," Oliver says and steps back with the bouquet still in his hand.

Annie hesitates a moment, then pulls her cell phone from her pocket and snaps a picture of him holding the flowers. She checks that it is good then gives a pleased nod. "I'll show it to Ophelia. That way she'll get to see the flowers and know we're both here."

When Annie enters the room Ophelia's eyes are open, and she is propped in an almost upright position.

"You look much better today," Annie says cheerfully; then she crosses over and kisses the wrinkled cheek.

This is partially true. Ophelia's color is better, but she appears almost frail lying in the bed. Today she looks her age because the feistiness is missing.

Annie waits until the nurse's back is turned, then pulls the jar of tea from her purse, slips a straw into it and holds it to Ophelia's lips.

"This is the healing blend," Annie whispers. "Take a few sips; it'll make you feel better."

Ophelia smiles.

SHE KNOWS THE BLEND WELL. She mixed it for Tom Kelly after Claudia died. In the weeks after Claudia was laid to rest, his sorrow gave him the look of a walking ghost. He came into the apothecary asking for a headache remedy, but Ophelia could see a headache was not his problem. Heartache was.

"What you need is a tonic," she told him.

That's when she created the healing mix. Tom Kelly drank that tea morning, noon and night, and within the year he was chipper enough to marry Alice Marie Higgins, the widow who lived two blocks over.

OPHELIA TILTS HER HEAD FORWARD and drinks from the straw that is offered. After a few sips, she looks up and smiles.

"Good," she says.

Annie stands beside the bed and takes Ophelia's hand in hers. "Do you remember what happened yesterday?"

For a moment Ophelia's expression is one of puzzlement; then she nods. "I heard the bells and decided to go to church."

She hesitates a bit, and Annie knows she is trying to remember.

"Do you recall getting in the car?" she asks.

"Yes." Ophelia's lips curl on one side, and she again nods. "At first the car wouldn't start, but after a few tries it did. Sometimes you've just got to—"

Annie cuts in. "Why?"

"I don't know why. I suppose it was because I pumped the gas pedal a few times, and then—"

"I'm not asking why the car started," Annie says. "I'm asking why you were behind the wheel."

Ophelia pinches her eyebrows together in an expression of disbelief. "Well, I would think that's obvious. To drive to church."

Annie gives an exasperated sigh. "But you haven't driven in over a year; why would you decide to do it now?"

"Because I wanted to go to church," Ophelia repeats. She pulls the tray closer and takes a few more sips of the tea. "This is quite tasty. Bring some more next time you come."

Before she can pursue their argument about the car, Annie spies the nurse headed for Ophelia's room. She grabs the jar of tea, slaps the lid on it and stuffs it back in her bag.

BY THE END OF THE DAY Annie has visited Ophelia seven times, and each time she has smuggled in the healing tea. When one jar is emptied, she produces another and ultimately even a third.

At dinnertime a volunteer carries in a tray and asks if Ophelia is up to trying a few bites.

"Actually I'm quite hungry," Ophelia replies.

She finishes everything on the tray except the beets.

"I never did like beets," she says. "But I could go for a bit more of that vanilla pudding."

That evening Annie stays for over a half-hour before the CCU guardian shoos her out.

"I'll be back in the morning," she promises.

WHEN ANNIE RETURNS TUESDAY MORNING, she goes directly to Ophelia's room. The bed is empty with clean sheets tucked tight around the edges.

She feels her heart slam against her chest, and her knees buckle. As she grabs for the foot of the bed, the watch-tapping nurse steps into the room.

"Looking for someone?" the nurse asks. For the first time she is smiling.

"Please don't tell me..." Annie can't get the rest of the words out.

"You don't want me to tell you that your grandma has been moved to the recovery unit on the second floor?"

Annie's face is flooded with relief. Without stopping to think about it, she grabs the nurse and hugs her.

"Thank you," she gushes. "Thank you, thank you, thank you!"

ON THE SECOND FLOOR VISITING hours are far more relaxed. Guests are permitted to come and go throughout the day. All day. Annie remains beside Ophelia for the entire afternoon. She is there when Doctor Milburn makes his rounds and stops in Ophelia's room.

He smiles. "Well, you're looking a lot better."

"I'm feeling better too," Ophelia replies.

"Good." He nods. "With this kind of progress, you'll be out of here before the end of the week."

She grins. "I can't wait. It'll be good to get home."

He glances up from the chart. "You're not going home. You're going to the Kipling Rehabilitation Center for a minimum of six and possibly eight weeks."

"What?" Ophelia exclaims. "I certainly am not!"

"You don't have a choice," he says. "You had a close call, and before I'm ready to let you go home I'm going to make sure your heart's strong enough to handle it."

"My heart is fine," Ophelia argues. "I had an episode, one small episode, that's all. It's nothing to worry about."

Doctor Milburn corrects her. "It *is* something to worry about. You had a major heart attack." The deadpan look on his face leaves no opening for an argument.

Annie slips him a sly smile. She knows this is one Ophelia will lose, and she is thankful for that.

Ophelia doesn't give up easily. "I have a business to run, a garden to—"

He stops her before she goes any further. "No, you don't. When you finish with rehab, you'll still have certain restrictions. No strenuous exercise, no lifting, no climbing stairs and definitely no driving!"

Ophelia folds her arms across her chest and glares at the doctor. "I told you, I have a business to run and a garden to take care of!"

"Well, you'll just have to get someone else to handle it for you."

"There is no one else!"

Doctor Milburn rubs his chin as if he is thinking this over. "I can't be absolutely certain," he says with a chuckle, "but I'll bet this pretty granddaughter of yours would be willing to help out."

"No," Ophelia says flatly. "She's a newlywed, and they're ready to go off on their honeymoon in—"

"Oh, pshaw," Annie says, laughing. "Oliver and I can go on a honeymoon anytime."

Ophelia glares over at Annie. "Hush up."

In the end, nothing Ophelia says sways Doctor Milburn's opinion. When she leaves the hospital she is going to the rehab center, and that's that.

ANNIE'S PLAN

The moment Doctor Milburn is out of the room, Ophelia looks at Annie and says, "You shouldn't have said anything. Maybe I could have convinced him to let me go home."

Annie laughs again. "You were never going to convince him. Anyway, I want you back at Memory House as much as you want to be there, but right now it really isn't the best thing."

"Who's to say what's best?" Ophelia grumbles.

"In this case the doctor. He wants to make sure you get well." Annie smiles. "And so do I."

"Oliver's not going to like this," Ophelia warns.

"He's fine with it. We've already discussed it."

"What about the library?"

"Giselle is back to full time now. I'll ask her to let me take a leave of absence."

"I don't know," Ophelia says mournfully. "I still think you and Oliver need to settle in a place of your own and have time to yourself." She hesitates a moment, and a smile slides onto her face. "I remember how it was when Edward and I were first married…"

Annie leans into the conversation as Ophelia tells of those first years with Edward.

"On lazy mornings we'd lie in bed for hours," she says. "We weren't doing a thing but enjoying the closeness of one another."

She continues, telling of Sunday afternoon picnics, evenings of lying beneath the stars and dreaming of all the places they would one day visit.

"Edward was a dreamer," she says, "and the wonder of it was that he took me to all those places with his words."

A smile lights Ophelia's face as she tells of how she could close her eyes and see the bookstalls of Paris or the brilliance of spring tulips stretching across the countryside of Holland.

In the middle of hearing about the bazaars of Morocco, Annie gives a nostalgic sigh. "Imagine, Edward traveling to all those places."

Ophelia chuckles. "He didn't travel to any of those places. He read books about them."

"Books?"

Ophelia nods. "He'd go to the library and check out a book on some place like Egypt. Then he'd come home and say, 'Opie, put on your dreaming cap, because this weekend we're off to visit the pyramids.'"

Ophelia's eyes sparkle as she laughs. "Opie. Edward was the only one who ever called me that."

"The two of you created such beautiful memories," Annie says wistfully.

Ophelia turns, and the magic is gone from her face.

"You're absolutely right," she says sternly, "and we wouldn't have had any of them if my mama had moved in with us."

Before Annie can challenge such a thought, Ophelia adds, "Not that I didn't love Mama. I loved her dearly. But if she'd have been there I would have been seeing to her every need instead of allowing myself time to dream alongside Edward."

"Oh, I don't think one thing has anything to do with the other," Annie says.

"It certainly does," Ophelia argues. "There are only so many hours in a day and so many days in a lifetime. A woman has got to decide how she wants to spend those hours and days."

Annie laughs. "Nonsense. There's time enough for everything."

"Not always," Ophelia replies sadly. "Not always."

For a moment she sits silently then explains that this is the reason Annie must treasure her early years with Oliver.

"In a few years you and Oliver will have a family, and the days will be crowded with things waiting to be done. You won't have the luxury of time to sit and dream together."

Annie smiles at such a thought. A family is what she's been wishing for all these years. She relishes the idea of a laundry basket filled with bibs and rompers.

"And when we've got those babies that are going to keep us so busy," she says, "don't you think they'll need a grandma?"

"I'm not suggesting I won't be part of your life; I'm just saying I don't want to be the biggest part," Ophelia argues.

FOR MOST OF THE AFTERNOON they go back and forth on the issue, but Annie stands firm in her resolution. She and Oliver will move into her old room at Memory House, and she will take care of everything until Ophelia is strong enough to return.

There is no mention of what will happen then, but a plan is already churning through Annie's mind.

WHEN ANNIE ARRIVES HOME FROM the hospital, Oliver is gone

and there is a note on the table. It says Andrew is picking him up, and he will be at the office if she needs him. He writes that he will be home about seven.

Perfect, she thinks.

She takes Ophelia's apron from the drawer, pulls it over her head and starts working. Tonight she will serve roasted chicken with vegetables from the garden and for dessert fresh raspberries with clotted cream.

It is fifteen minutes before seven when she hears the chugging of a car pulling into the drive.

When Oliver walks into the house he is carrying a chilled bottle of champagne and three red roses tied with a ribbon.

"Since you didn't get to enjoy the special dinner I had planned," he says, "I thought I'd make this one special."

"I had the same thought," Annie says, laughing. "I've made—"

"Roast chicken," he says, finishing her sentence. "I could smell it the minute I opened the door."

Annie has set the tiny table on the back porch with the china that once belonged to Edward's mama, and in the center of the table five narrow candles bunch together on a crystal butter dish.

When they sit down to dinner Annie can easily imagine this is exactly how it was with Ophelia and Edward. She mentions this to Oliver.

"Perhaps we're following in the footsteps of their memories," she says.

"Only temporarily," he says. "When we get back to Wyattsville, we'll start making our own memories."

It is only now that Annie tells him Ophelia won't be coming home for more than a month.

"And when she does," Annie says, "she won't be able to climb stairs or drive."

A look of disappointment tugs at Oliver's face.

"I'm sorry," Annie says. "I realize this isn't ideal, but Ophelia doesn't have anyone else. I have to be here to run the apothecary and care for her."

"I know," he replies sadly. "As much as I wish it were different, I wouldn't change you for anything in the world. That big heart of yours may be a pain in the neck, but it's also why I love you as I do."

He stretches his arm across the table and lifts her hand into his. "We'll work it out."

Oliver is uncertain as to how they will work it out, but he knows that wherever Annie is he will be beside her. Never before has he loved a woman the way he loves Annie.

AFTER DINNER THEY TAKE THE comforter out to the lawn and lie beneath the stars. A slight breeze ripples across the pond, and from the far end of the water they can hear the nasal honking of the swans. Annie pulls her iPod from her pocket and selects her easy listening collection.

When Eric Clapton's *Wonderful Tonight* plays, they dance barefoot on the grass. Their bodies are so close and sway in such unison that at a distance you'd believe them to be one figure. Her head is pressed to his chest, and he can smell the sweetness of jasmine in her hair.

"I love you, Annie," he whispers, then tilts her face to his and kisses her full on the mouth.

Afterward they lie side by side on the comforter and talk about the future. Oliver promises when the time is right they will take their honeymoon. And then one day start a family and have a home of their own.

"With a big backyard," he says. "A really big yard, one with room for a garden and a sandbox and a swing."

Of course all of this is in the future. For now there is only the reality of living in a small bedroom. A bedroom that is across the hall from what will soon be Ophelia's room. And the three of them will share a single bathroom.

With a bit of sadness threaded through her words, Annie says, "I just hate that Ophelia won't be able to lie in bed and look at the stars. I know that's something she'll miss."

She tells some of the stories Ophelia has told her.

"Imagine," she says, "Edward knew the name of all these stars."

This thought gives Oliver an idea.

OPHELIA

Annie means well, but sometimes she can be as bull-headed as I am. She's set on the thought that she's gonna take care of me when I come home, but I'm just as determined that she won't.

I may be getting on in years, but I'm not too old to remember what it's like being young and newly married. Why, I wouldn't trade those early years with Edward for anything in the world. If the good Lord came to me tonight and said I could live another century if I was willing to forget those first years, I'd turn Him down flat.

A man and woman need time to get to know one another. To explore each other's bodies, make love and dance around the living room naked if they want to. Two people married in the sight of God ought to be able to do things like that without worrying some old biddy is going to hear them.

I'm fine with having Annie and Oliver stay at Memory House while I'm at the rehab center since they have the place to themselves. But once I come home I'm gonna insist they go on back to their own house.

I'll say having them underfoot all the time is a nuisance. If Annie keeps harping on me about not staying alone, I'll tell her I'm going to get Edna Porter's sister to come live with me in exchange for free room and board. I won't really do it, because Maggie talks nonstop and I'm not

43

sure how long I'd be able to put up with that. I'll just say it so Annie can put her mind to ease.

I'll say it's okay if she wants to work in the apothecary and lets me pay her the same salary she makes at the library. That would be good for both of us. She'd have her own life with Oliver, and I'd still have time to sit and talk with her.

It's funny how Annie fills up that big hole in my heart. The house seems downright lonely when she's not there. Memories are a big comfort, but there are times when you just need a live friend to talk and laugh with.

I think Edward would be pleased to know I have that.

Ophelia

THE ARCHITECT

On the Friday that Ophelia is scheduled to be moved to the Kipling Rehabilitation Center, Annie wakes up early. She goes to the loft and packs a suitcase with the things Ophelia has asked her to bring: the blue robe, three cotton nightgowns, some housecoats and an assortment of creams, lotions and powders.

At the last minute she includes the Lannigan Bible and a snow globe that once belonged to the Lannigan girl. The Bible holds the first memory Ophelia ever discovered, and it is one of her favorite treasures.

When Annie is ready to leave she kisses Oliver goodbye and says, "I'll call you later."

"Call me here," he replies. "I'm not going into the office today."

Were this another time, a time when Annie didn't have so much on her mind, she likely would have asked why, but today she doesn't. Instead she hurries out the door so she will get to the hospital early.

OLIVER HAS SAID NOTHING ABOUT his plan, but for the past two days he has thought about little else. Not because he minds the daily commute to Wyattsville, but because the door to the other bedroom is less than three feet from the door to their room. As much as he cares for Ophelia, that's too close for comfort.

Since the day Annie first appeared on his doorstep, Oliver has wanted to make love to her. Not in a cautious way that hides beneath the covers and speaks in soft whispers to avoid being heard, but with a joyous passion that casts abandon aside.

Today he has three different architects coming to look at the house. His thought is to add a wing, one that is an exact replica of the loft, skylight and all.

The first one arrives at ten o'clock on the button. He checks the loft then walks through the remainder of the house.

"What you need is a completely new floor plan," he says. "If we take down the wall between the living room and the dining area, we can create a pass-through to the kitchen and make it a great room."

"We're happy with the house just as it is," Oliver replies. "All we need is a wing for the extra bedroom."

The architect raises an eyebrow. "And you want it to look like that room upstairs?"

Oliver nods.

"That room looks like something a do-it-yourselfer put together. It's not finished properly. There's no beveling on the bookcase. The mitering on the baseboard is crooked as a drunkard's hat, and I'll bet dollars to doughnuts that if you took a level to the floor you'd find at least a seven degree slant."

"You've got a good piece of property here," he says. "Just give me the okay, and I can turn this place into a showcase with nice clean contemporary lines. I'm visualizing an all glass walk-through that leads to a side wing suite."

"I'm not interested in redoing the house," Oliver repeats. "All I want is a wing that replicates the upstairs bedroom."

The architect wrinkles his nose and shakes his head. "Sorry, buddy, no can do. I've got a reputation to uphold."

He takes back the business card lying on the table and walks out.

THE SECOND ARCHITECT IS NO better, the only difference being he suggests taking down the wall between the two bedrooms and making it one large suite.

"That doesn't solve my problem," Oliver says.

"Well, I'm thinking bump out that upstairs room, double the size and add a full bath. That way you'd have three decent-sized bedrooms."

This time Oliver is the one to shake his head. "That's not going to work."

The architect hands him a card and suggests he think it over.

"Another full bath will definitely increase the value of the house," he says.

THE LAST APPOINTMENT IS WITH Max Martinelli. When Oliver opens the door he is surprised to see a woman—one who is better described as a young girl.

She sticks her arm out and offers her hand. "Max Martinelli."

Oliver shakes the offered hand and invites her in. After a moment of awkward hesitation he says, "Your listing said Max, so I thought you'd be a guy."

She laughs. "I know. That's why I use Max instead of Maxine. Not too many people are interested in working with a female architect, especially one who's fresh out of school."

"What school?"

"Parson's Design."

"Can't argue with that," Oliver says. "So let's see what you've learned."

He guides Max up the stairs and shows her the loft. "What I want to do is add a wing for an extra bedroom that's an exact replica of this room. Skylight and all."

"I can see why," she says. "Feels like there's a lot of love in this room."

"Feels like?"

She nods. "If you open yourself up, you can feel the parts of life that have been lived in a room. Say you had a spare bedroom used for an office and took all the furniture out; I'd still know it had been an office. Work places have a crinkly feeling; there's lots of left-over frustrations and disappointments in the walls."

Oliver chuckles. "My wife and Ophelia are going to love you."

Without stopping to think about it, Oliver begins explaining how Annie came to his door saying she'd found a memory in an old bicycle that once belonged to his dad.

"It was a pretty unbelievable story," he says, laughing, "but one look at those eyes of hers, and I honestly didn't care."

Without batting an eyelash, Max says, "Unbelievable, why?"

Oliver raises an eyebrow and looks at her curiously. "Unbelievable because it's not likely a person will find a memory left behind. It's not exactly a dime lost between the sofa cushions."

Max laughs. "It's not like that at all. You don't actually *find* a memory, you just sort of sense it's been there. It's an aura people leave behind. Some are more powerful than others; those are the ones that are easier to feel."

"An aura?"

"You know, like an invisible fingerprint. It tells you who the person was and how they felt about things."

Although there is a look of doubt on Oliver's face she continues.

"That's how I knew there was a lot of love in this room." She smiles. "That and noticing a lot of the woodwork was done by someone with more love than skill."

"Ophelia's husband built this room."

"I thought so." Max runs her hand along the bed platform and looks up. "Was he an astronomer?"

"No, a businessman. But from what Ophelia has told us, he was fascinated with the stars and knew most of them by name."

"I knew it," Max says.

"By the aura he left?"

She gives a sheepish grin and nods. "That...and the way the skylight is positioned directly over the bed. If you pay attention to such things, you can learn a lot about a person."

"Good grief," Oliver says. "You remind me so much of Annie. You even look like her."

Max laughs. "I do, except her eyes are violet and mine are green." She lifts her head and gives him a bug-eyed look. "Green, see?"

"You can tell the color of a person's eyes from an aura?"

"No. I met Annie at the library. I was checking out a book on extra sensory perceptions, and we got to talking. She told me that same story about the bicycle, so I kind of figured it had to be the same person."

Oliver shakes his head. "Unbelievable."

"Actually, no, it's not. We do look a lot alike, so I can see why you'd think..."

MAX MARTINELLI

This is almost too good to be true. The minute I walked into this house I could feel the history of it. It's not super fancy, but it's full of charm. It's the kind of place where you want to walk around sniffing the wood and peeking behind the curtains.

Those bookcases in the loft are fifty years old if they're a day. You don't find that kind of grainy oak anywhere nowadays, except maybe in a mansion where some hot shot has paid through the nose to get it.

The truth is I would have designed the wing for half of what Oliver Doyle is paying me. Actually I'd have done it for free it I had to. A project like this is great in an architect's portfolio. It shows you've got style. I mean real style, not a cookie-cutter version of glass and chrome style.

It's funny that a judge is married to Annie from the library. But it's even funnier to hear him say she thinks like I do.

When Annie told me that bicycle story I guessed she was a lot like me. If it was up to me I would have stayed and talked to her all day, but you know how it is in a library. There were people behind me waiting to check out, so I just said I'd see her next time.

Maybe when the first sketches are ready I'll come by in the evening *when she's at home. I'll bring a bottle of wine and say let's have a toast or something.*

It would be a good way to start up a friendship.

This is so absolutely cool. Landing a project like this is like winning the architectural lottery.

ROOMMATES

On Friday morning Ophelia is taken to the Kipling Rehabilitation Center in an ambulance. No siren, no flashing lights. Just a rock hard gurney to transport her from one bed to another. Annie is not allowed to ride in the ambulance. She will follow along in her own car.

When they arrive at the center, the attendant lifts the gurney from the ambulance and rolls it into a foyer. He hands the waiting orderly a sheath of papers and says, "Browne, Ophelia."

Moments later she is whooshed into an elevator, taken to the second floor and assigned to room 214. On the wall outside the entrance to the room there are two patient nameplates: Lillian Markowitz is 214A, Ophelia is 214B.

As they move her from the gurney to the bed, Ophelia catches a quick glimpse of the other bed and gives a saddened sigh. She'd hoped to have a spot next to the window, a place where on sleepless nights she could gaze at the stars and know Edward was with her. Instead she is on the inside with a divider curtain on one side and a wall on the other.

Lillian Markowitz has the bed beside Ophelia's window. She is a woman with fire engine red fingernails, hair the color of a canary and a laugh that could easily be mistaken for the sound of a hyena. Already she has crowded the windowsill with pots of flowers and looped a dozen or more get well cards over the slats of the venetian blind. Only a few thin slivers of sunlight can now slide through.

Ophelia knows that for however long she is here, she will not see the stars. For her, that is reason enough to be out of here as quickly as possible.

When Jeanne, the day nurse, comes with the water pitcher and welcome packet, Ophelia says, "I'm ready to get started with my therapy."

Jeanne chuckles. "You're not scheduled for therapy until Monday."

Ophelia slumps back into the pillows. "Monday?" Her disappointment is obvious.

A voice from the other side of the curtain calls out, "Count your blessings, honey."

At first Ophelia is not sure if the woman is talking to her or someone else. "Excuse me?"

"I said count your blessings!" Lillian calls again, her voice a bit louder this time. "Those therapists are nice fellas, but they work your tail off!"

"Are you talking to me?" Ophelia asks.

"Of course I'm talking to you," Lillian replies. "There's nobody else here."

Before Ophelia has a chance to answer, the telephone on the other side of the curtain rings.

Lillian lifts the receiver and yells, "Hello."

She is still on the telephone when Annie arrives.

"Sorry I took so long," Annie says. "I had to park in the back lot." She leans in, kisses Ophelia's cheek and whispers, "Have you met your roommate yet?"

Ophelia shakes her head and gives a mischievous grin. She

lowers her voice to a thin whisper and says, "I'm not sure I want to."

"Gotcha." Annie nods. She moves to the divider curtain and speaks in a voice that can be heard over Lillian's laughter. "Perhaps your roommate would like some privacy."

She reaches out and starts to give the curtain a tug.

"No need to close that!" Lillian hollers. "This ain't private."

Annie pokes her head around to the other side. "You sure?"

Lillian nods and keeps on talking. "If I was Bertha…"

Her voice fills the room. It is the kind of sound that bounces back and echoes in your ears. The call lasts until two visitors arrive; then she says, "Sorry, Martha, I've gotta go. Sadie and Sam are here."

The caller obviously has more to say because Lillian replies, "Yeah, yeah, I'll tell them. No, I'm not gonna forget…"

Only after Sadie approaches the bed and pulls Lillian into her ample bosom does the phone call finally end.

"That Martha," Lillian says with a groan. "She can go on forever."

ANNIE AGAIN POKES HER HEAD around the partially drawn curtain and asks, "Would you like me to close this so you can have some privacy with your visitors?"

Lillian gives a raucous peal of laughter and shakes her head. "Honey, I ain't needed privacy since Walter died in nineteen ninety-nine. Sadie and Sam are just friends from Baylor."

The couple acknowledges their introduction with a polite nod.

Lillian eyes Annie and asks, "What'd you say your name was, honey?"

"Annie…um, Doyle."

Lillian waves her hand toward the divider. "Push that back a bit further, will you, sweetie?"

Once the curtain is back as far as it will go, Lillian leans forward and smiles at Ophelia. "We're roomies, so I guess we ought to get to know one another. I'm Lillian Markowitz, but you can call me Lil. And you?"

"Ophelia Browne."

The woman is loud and brassy, not at all the type Ophelia would choose for a friend, and yet she cannot help liking her. For a split second she even thinks of saying, "You can call me Opie," but that moment slides by and she doesn't.

Once the introductions are done, the awkwardness of a new friendship eases and the void is filled with conversation. Ophelia joins in little by little. At first it is only a word here and there, but before long she is chuckling at Sam's jokes and egging him on to tell another.

Ophelia is in the middle of telling how she'd revived a geranium that was good as dead when the orderly comes with a wheelchair.

"Time for therapy, Miz Lillian," he says.

Keeping her eyes fixed on Ophelia, Lillian waves him off. "Hold up a minute, sweetie, I wanna hear the end of this."

When Ophelia concludes with directions on how to shake the dirt loose from a geranium's roots and transplant it, Lillian starts to climb from the bed. "I gotta remember that."

The orderly steadies Lillian as she climbs into the chair. Once she is settled she reaches back and taps his arm. "Okay, sweetie, I'm good to go."

"Miz Lillian, why you keep calling me sweetie?" he says with a laugh. "I done told you my name is Tyrone."

Lillian looks up at him and winks. "You think I don't know that? I call you sweetie 'cause I like you. If I didn't like you, well, then…" She lets go of a laugh that lingers even after she has left the room.

IT SURPRISES ANNIE WHEN SAM and Sadie stay after Lillian is gone. It is nearing four when they stand and get ready to leave. Sadie comes to the side of the bed and pulls Ophelia into her bosom just as she did Lillian.

"Sam's got a dentist appointment, so we won't be here tomorrow," she says. "But we'll be back the day after."

Sadie loops her arm through Sam's, and they leave together.

As Ophelia listens to the click-clack of their footsteps disappearing down the hall, she looks up at Annie and says, "This isn't going to be nearly as bad as I thought."

She leans back into the pillow and yawns. Moments later her eyes close, and within minutes she is fast asleep.

Annie tiptoes out of the room then stops and glances back. Ophelia is snoring lightly, but the corner of her mouth is curled into a smile.

THE MAGIC OF FRIENDSHIP

Oliver is showing Max through the remainder of the house when the front door clicks open and Annie calls out.

"We're in the kitchen," he answers.

Annie is home earlier than expected, and she has already seen the unfamiliar car in the driveway. At first she'd assumed it was an apothecary customer, but Oliver's answer didn't make sense. *We're in the kitchen?* Why would an apothecary customer be in the kitchen?

As she enters the room Annie sees him holding onto the arm of a girl who looks vaguely familiar. The girl steps down from the stool she is standing on and turns. When Annie sees her face, she recognizes the girl immediately.

"Max?" she says.

Max nods then crosses the room and sticks out her hand. "Hi, how are you?"

Annie takes the hand that is offered. "I think I'm good," she answers cautiously. Confusion wrinkles her brow as she asks, "What are you doing here?"

Without waiting for Max to answer, Oliver speaks up. "This was going to be a surprise, but since you caught us..." He explains his plan for adding a room to the house.

At this point, Max jumps in.

"Recreating the loft is a stroke of genius," she says enthusiastically. "If we position the room on the left side of the house, I can add an extra window that overlooks the garden, and with no tree overhang Ophelia will have a clear view of the night sky."

Still looking puzzled, Annie asks, "What do you mean recreating the loft?"

Oliver again answers. "I thought if we make the new addition exactly like the loft, Ophelia wouldn't feel such a sense of loss. It would be like the room she had but without the stairs." He gives a sheepish grin. "Not to mention the fact that it would give us a lot more privacy."

Annie's smile is almost too big for her face. She kisses Oliver and then turns to Max. "Didn't I tell you I was marrying the sweetest man in the world?"

"You sure did," Max laughs. "You sure did."

Moments later they are deep in conversation about Max's thoughts for the extension.

"I can see why you want to preserve the integrity of the house," she says. "It's absolutely beautiful." She hesitates a moment then adds, "It seems to have a hidden history."

"Have you seen the apothecary?" Annie asks.

"No, but I'd love to."

Max follows Annie through the hallway and into the tiny front room. The moment they step inside the apothecary she gives a deep sigh and remains there breathing in the scents of lavender and spice. After a few moments she moves to the table and touches her hand to the basket of potpourri. She turns and smiles. "This isn't the same as the one in the hallway, is it?"

Annie shakes her head. "This is lavender grown in the garden."

Before she can explain Ophelia's special potpourri, Max says, "The one in the hallway changes scent, doesn't it?"

"Oh, my gosh," Annie says. "I can't believe you noticed."

"When I first came in I thought it was strange that a potpourri would smell like drawing paper; then as we went past it just now I caught a whiff of burgundy wine."

Annie explains that Ophelia's special mix takes on the smell of whatever a person is thinking of.

"When you got here you were probably focused on drawings for the job," she says, "but now I'm guessing it's time for a glass of wine." She laughs and asks if Max would like to join them for dinner.

"I'd love to," Max answers. "But can we just stay here a few minutes longer?"

When Annie nods, Max walks around the room touching her fingers to the bottles, jars and baskets. "There are so many different auras in this room."

Annie thinks back on the endless stream of customers who have come and gone through the shop. "Can you feel all the people who have been here?"

"Not individually," Max says, "but certain groups."

"Wow." Annie shakes her head in amazement, then says she has no such power. "If it wasn't for Ophelia, I would have never thought to look for memories."

She hesitates, touches her chin then smiles. It is as if Annie is calling up her own memories. They are right there, just beneath the surface of her skin.

Max senses them. "I know how you feel about Ophelia, and I promise to make this new room as wonderful as the loft."

Annie laughs. "Edward built that room for Ophelia, and I doubt—"

"Don't be so sure," Max says and then shares the plans that have been running through her head since she viewed the room.

"I'm thinking we can pull the bookcases and platform bed out of the loft and reuse them in the new room. Those things have the essence of the years they spent together, and they're chock full of memories—"

Annie's eyes open wide. "Essence, like smell?"

"I don't know if I'd say smell," Max replies. "It's more like a feeling. You stand next to that platform, and you can almost see them in the bed together."

Again Annie shakes her head in amazement. "You have a real talent, like Ophelia does. Who taught you?"

Max shrugs. "No one. I studied design in Paris during my second year. During that year I'd go to one of the old buildings and sit in the lobby for hours trying to get the inspiration of the place. Then one day I started hearing far away conversations." She laughs. "At first I thought it was because I had really good hearing, but when I focused on the words I realized I was hearing things that had been said fifty years earlier."

Annie stands mesmerized.

"Oliver claims you can do pretty much the same thing," Max says.

"Nowhere near it," Annie says. "I was lucky enough to discover Oliver's daddy's memories, but not much more."

She doesn't mention the locket. The memory inside the locket is filled with heartache and pain. The mention of it is too fearful. It is better to believe it never existed.

"But what about here in the apothecary—"

Annie cuts in. "I only know how to mix the things Ophelia taught me. Mostly cures for different problems and ailments. It's not really magic. People think it is, but it's not."

"Well, if people believe it, isn't that a sort of magic in itself?"

Annie shakes her head. "When a broken heart is healed or someone falls in love, it's not because of anything I give them. It happens because the person has the courage to believe in what they're hoping for. The truth is they heal themselves, but they probably wouldn't be brave enough to try without what they think is a magic potion."

Max nods as if she understands, but the truth is she knows differently. She feels the magic of this place. "I'm just getting started in this business. You think you could mix up something to help me find new clients?"

Annie smiles at the thought. She knows that despite Max's extraordinary abilities to sense things, she wants to believe in the magic of the apothecary just as all the others do.

"Sure," Annie says and pulls the mulling cup from the shelf.

ANNIE

When Ophelia first told me about her ability to find memories, I thought it was the strangest thing ever. But now I'm starting to believe any number of people might have it. They just never discover it because they don't know to look for it.

Max has found hers, that's for sure. She stayed for dinner last night and while we were talking about something else entirely, I could feel her thinking about how she was going to design the new room.

I can't help but like Max, and I'm sure she feels the same about me. When she left, she gave me her business card and on the back she wrote her cell phone number. She said to give her a call and we'd have lunch. I'm going to do it, because I like the idea of having her for a friend.

I'd love to introduce her to Ophelia, but I'm going to wait until she has the drawings ready. I can't even begin to imagine the look on Ophelia's face when she finds out Oliver is doing this for her.

Oliver is truly the most thoughtful and kindest man in the world. He's a lot like his daddy, which is a good thing. Ethan seems so sweet you'd think sugar wouldn't melt in his mouth, but I've heard stories of what he was like as a kid and there's a whole lot of devilment underneath all that niceness.

Oliver is that way too. When he holds my hand I can feel the *sweetness of his love shimmying up my arm, but when he kisses me the way he did the other night on the lawn the excitement just about curls my toes. Times like that I want to jump out of my clothes and say,* Take me, I'm all yours.

Being here in this house, I often imagine Ophelia and Edward doing the same things Oliver and I do. That night when we were outside and danced on the lawn, I could almost picture them dancing just like we did. The funny thing is in my mind Edward looked exactly like Oliver.

That can't possibly be...can it?

In the Weeks that Follow

As it turns out, Ophelia is right. Being at the Kipling Rehabilitation Center is far better than she'd anticipated. Before a week has passed, she and Lillian have become fast friends.

Lillian tells stories of how for over a year she'd danced on the stage of Radio City Music Hall in the line of Rockettes.

"I was third from the end," she says. "Barbara Ann Malloy was smack in the center."

Her thoughts roll back through time, and a touch of envy surfaces. "I always wanted to be in the center," she says, "but I wasn't tall enough."

Ophelia hangs on every word, and when Lillian tells how she marched in Macy's Thanksgiving Day parade Ophelia sighs in admiration.

"Such an exciting life," she says.

Lillian cackles. "It sounds more exciting than it was. The truth is we damn near froze our butts off that day. When they asked for volunteers the next year, I didn't even raise my hand."

When Ophelia tells of her life, there is a glistening in her eyes.

It is almost impossible to know if it is the spark of remembrance or the start of tears.

"The most exciting thing that ever happened to me was marrying Edward," she says. She tells of how they would lie in the grass on summer evenings and look at the stars.

"Can you believe he knew almost every one of them by name?"

"I'd believe it of Edward, but not Walter," Lillian replies. "Walter mostly liked bowling. Bowling's not nearly as romantic as watching stars."

Ophelia continues and tells how Edward finished the loft and added a skylight.

"When winter came, we'd cuddle under our comforter and lie there and look up at the stars the same as we did in summer." She hesitates a moment then shares what she has shared with very few others. "Even now I get great solace from looking into the night sky. Silly as it may seem, I can see my Edward up there. He's looking down and watching over me."

That same day Lillian insists they change beds.

"I don't care a bean about looking at the night sky," she says, "and it's downright annoying when the morning sun pokes me in the eye."

AS THE WEEKS SLIDE BY Ophelia's days are filled with activity from morning to night. Lillian's friends become her friends, and when she is not being hauled off to therapy they play pinochle.

By the third week Ophelia has made such progress that she is allowed to get out of bed and walk around on her own. On a quiet afternoon when there are no visitors, she and Lillian thump their walkers down the hallway and sit in the sunroom laughing at the *The Ellen Degeneres Show*.

"This television thing is quite amusing," Ophelia says. She confesses that she's never had a television and never had the desire to own one.

"Until now," she adds.

"No television?" Lillian says. "What'd you do for entertainment?"

"In the early years Edward and I spent our evenings together. We'd go for walks and picnics, feed the ducks on the pond, count stars..." She gives a shy giggle. "...and make love."

Lillian laughs. "That was over sixty years ago. What about now?"

"Well," Ophelia says hesitantly. "I have the bed and breakfast guests to take care of, and the apothecary, and the garden always needs something done—"

"All that's work!" Lillian snaps. "What do you do for fun?"

It is a full minute before Ophelia answers. "I read books, or Annie and I sit on the back porch and talk."

"Annie's a young woman. Don't you have any friends your own age?"

Ophelia thinks for a moment then says, "A number of apothecary customers are my age. Herman Harris is older!"

"They're customers," Lillian argues, "not friends."

"But they're like friends."

"It's not the same. Do you go to their house and have coffee? Do they come over just to play pinochle?"

Ophelia has to admit they don't. "But that doesn't mean they're not friends," she adds.

Lillian rolls her eyes in a highly dramatic fashion. "You need to get a life."

"I have a life," Ophelia says sharply. "A fine life!" Then she stands, leaves Lillian sitting on the sofa in the sunroom and starts thumping her walker toward the door.

"Living with old memories and a young girl to take care of

you is not a fine life," Lillian calls out. "It's just sitting around waiting to die!"

Ophelia hears but doesn't turn around or answer as she angrily thumps her way back to the room. Before she climbs into the bed she yanks the divider curtain closed.

THAT AFTERNOON WHEN SAM AND Pauline come to play pinochle, Ophelia says she's not in the mood.

"Not in the mood?" Sam says. "After you've won the last two times?"

"Pay no attention," Lillian tells him. "She's just pouting 'cause I told her the God's honest truth."

Pauline gives an exasperated sigh. "I swear, Lil, there's times when you ought to keep all that honesty to yourself."

AFTER SHE CLOSES THE APOTHECARY, Annie comes to visit. This is the first time she has seen the curtain drawn. She nods a quick hello to the pinochle players and hurries around to Ophelia's bedside.

"What's wrong?" she asks.

"Nothing," Ophelia replies. "I'm just not in the mood to socialize."

"Are you sick?" Annie puts her hand to Ophelia's forehead, but it's cool to the touch. "I don't think you have a fever. Is your stomach okay?"

"My stomach is fine."

"Well, then why—"

"I told you, I'm not in the mood to socialize."

"But for the past three weeks you've—"

"Do I have to explain every single thing?"

"You don't have to explain anything," Annie replies. "It just..."

Ophelia hears the hurt in her voice. She reaches out and places her hand atop Annie's.

"I'm sorry for being so crotchety," she says. "I think I'm a bit overtired tonight."

Annie gives a sympathetic smile. "Too much therapy?"

Ophelia nods. "I think so." She doesn't mention the sunroom incident.

Annie lifts Ophelia's head, plumps the pillow then eases her back into position. "How about if I read to you for a while? That might help you to relax."

"That would be nice."

Annie picks up the worn copy of *Rebecca* lying on the nightstand and starts to read. The stress of this day has been too much for Ophelia. Before long her eyes close, and she begins snoring softly.

Annie replaces the book on the nightstand and starts to tiptoe out. The pinochle players are gone and the overhead lights have been dimmed, but as she moves past the second bed Lillian speaks.

"You're not doing Ophelia any good," she says.

Annie stops and turns. "Are you talking to me?"

"Of course I am," Lillian says. "You're not doing Ophelia any good."

This statement takes Annie by surprise. "What are you talking about?"

"You mollycoddling her the way you do. That's not going to help her stand on her own and be happy."

"She doesn't need to stand on her own," Annie says angrily. "She's got me to take care of her!"

"Exactly!" Lillian comes back. "So when she goes home, she'll be an old woman lying in bed with you waiting on her hand and foot. Then she'll die!"

Annie gives a gasp that sounds as if she's been punched in the stomach. "How dare you! I love Ophelia and would never let something happen to her! Why, right now we're doing everything we can to make sure the house will be comfortable when she comes home."

"Oh, great," Lillian chides. "Then she can wallow in her memories and die even faster."

"You're intolerable!" Annie says, then turns on her heel and heads for the door.

"Maybe so," Lillian calls out, "but I'm also right!"

EVERY RIGHT

Lillian has a voice that at times can sound like a foghorn. Although Ophelia had dozed for a while, the sound of that foghorn woke her. She'd said nothing but listened to the entire conversation.

Annie has been gone for almost an hour when Ophelia finally climbs from the bed and pulls open the curtain. She looks Lillian in the eye and says, "You shouldn't have done that!"

"Done what?" Lillian replies. "Tell the truth?"

"It doesn't matter whether or not it's the truth; you have no right—"

"I have every right," Lillian cuts in. "I'm your friend."

"That doesn't give you—"

"Yes, it does," Lillian interrupts. "If I see you making a mistake and don't say something, then I'm not much of a friend."

Ophelia turns away, then hesitates and looks back. "What mistake am I making?"

"Expecting Annie to stay there and take care of you."

"I'm not expecting anything," Ophelia replies defensively. "I've asked her to work in the apothecary, that's all. I'm planning to hire someone for the other things. A live-in housekeeper, maybe."

"Ha!" Lillian sneers. The sound of it is like a slap in the face. "You know Annie won't let you do that; she loves you too much."

"Okay, suppose you're right; suppose she and Oliver do decide to stay there. I don't see what harm—"

"Pleeeaase!" Lillian groans. "You'll be a millstone around their neck. Don't you remember what it was like when you and Edward were first married?"

Ophelia remembers. She remembers it all. The warmth of lying together, the lazy Sunday mornings, making love in the kitchen, on the back porch and hidden in the dark shadows of the weeping willow.

Lillian doesn't wait for Ophelia to answer.

"If you love Annie," she says, "you'll give her the same chance at happiness you had."

Ophelia doesn't look back. She doesn't want Lillian to see the tears. Without saying anything more, she closes the divider curtain.

OPHELIA DOESN'T CLIMB INTO THE bed; instead she pulls the window shade up as high as it will go and sits in the chair. From here she can see most of the sky. The moon is full and bright, but she looks beyond it and searches for the familiar constellations. There in the midst of those stars she will find Edward, and this is a night when she needs to feel his nearness.

Tonight Ophelia's heart feels like a stone in her chest. It is as if everything she loves has been taken from her again. She replays Lillian's words over and over.

Don't you want to give her the same chance you had with Edward? she hears Lillian argue.

I am *giving her the same chance*, Ophelia tells herself. *I won't be a burden. I'll hire a housekeeper. I'll tell Annie she doesn't have to work in the apothecary unless it's what she wants. I'll explain that she owes me nothing, that she and Oliver are free to live their life as they will.*

Even after Ophelia has gone through all of these rationales, she cannot shake Lillian's words from her mind. *Annie will never accept that; she loves you too much.*

Tonight more than ever before, Ophelia wants Edward to come to her, to comfort her and give her the guidance she needs. She closes her eyes and tries to will him into being, but the best she can do is remember their days together.

She picks through her favorite memories. They are like pages of a much-loved book, worn and crumpled from use but never changing. Thinking back on that first Christmas, the night Edward unveiled the starlit loft he'd created for her, she can feel the warmth of his arms and the passion of his kisses. As she sits looking into the sky and praying that he will come, her eyes fill with water and tears fall.

ANNIE IS LOOKING UP AT the same sky. Oliver is already asleep when she slides from the bed and tiptoes out to the backyard. She spreads the comforter on the ground and sits. She also remembers Lillian's words.

Then she'll die.

She tries to picture the future but can see only happiness. Ophelia settled in the new room with her treasures surrounding her. *Wallow in memories? Impossible,* Annie tells herself. Ophelia loves those precious memories. They are a joy, not a burden.

A small voice in the back of her mind whispers, *Really?*

Really is a question Annie cannot answer. Only Ophelia knows the answer.

THE FIRST LIGHT OF DAY drifts into the sky as Annie returns to bed. By then she has decided she will ask Max to rush the drawing for the new room. Once she has shown the drawing to Ophelia, Annie believes she will be able to see the truth.

She will keep a close watch on Ophelia's expression, be aware of any telltale sign—a wrinkled brow, a saddened sigh, a twitching at the side of her mouth.

If that happens, Annie is uncertain what she will do. She cannot go and leave Ophelia to fend for herself; nor can she stay and have her wither away from lack of purpose.

There is no good answer. She can only pray that Oliver's recreation of the loft will bring Ophelia the happiness she deserves.

PERCHANCE TO DREAM

In time Ophelia becomes so weary that her head falls onto her chest. She then slides her feet from her slippers and reluctantly climbs into bed. The weight of Lillian's words is still heavy in her chest.

When sleep finally comes, Ophelia's memories become as real as the day they happened. It is a July night, a night too hot for sleep. She and Edward lie on the lawn, feeling the grass beneath them. An afternoon storm has soaked the ground, and the cool dampness is refreshing against her skin.

Edward sits up and leans over. He kisses her nose then his lips slide down to her mouth.

"It's too hot to sleep," he whispers.

She moves her mouth across his cheek and tastes the salt of his skin. Ophelia knows what he wants and giggles.

"Not here," she says. "Not out in the open."

He gives a hearty laugh, one that is fat and round, thick with happiness. He takes her hand and pulls her to her feet. With his kisses trailing across her bare shoulder and his arm wrapped around her waist, he guides her toward the willow.

She reaches out, pushes aside a handful of the drooping branches and they move into the shadows of the tree.

They lie on the ground and he kisses her, tenderly at first and then with a passion hot as fire. When he pulls her to his chest, she can feel the pulse of his heartbeat and it matches the rhythm of her own. She opens her eyes to see the beauty of his face, but what she sees is her mother standing in a tangle of willow branches with a disapproving look stretched across her face.

OPHELIA SCREAMS AND BOLTS INTO an upright position. Before she has dismissed the dream, Lillian is standing beside her bed.

"What's wrong?" Lillian asks. "Are you alright?"

For the moment Ophelia is too shaken to speak.

"Do you want me to call for a doctor?"

"No," Ophelia replies. "It was just a bad dream."

LILLIAN UNDERSTANDS HOW DREAMS CAN shake you to the core of your being. After Walter died she lived with them for almost two years. She'd come from the funeral back to the house they'd shared for the whole of their marriage, and there he was in every corner of every room. The smell of him still in the clothes left hanging in the closet. A smudge of paste stuck to his toothbrush. The toe of a slipper protruding from beneath the bed. A thousand times Lillian thought of clearing the place out, taking those perfectly good clothes to the Goodwill store so a needy person could make use of them. But she didn't.

Getting rid of Walter's things would be like watching him die all over again. Lillian doubted she could make it through such an ordeal. Besides, she had no need of an empty closet.

So for the full two years everything remained just as it was the day he died, and every night the dreams came. Long before daylight Lillian would awaken soaked with perspiration and tied down by a tangle of sheets.

Then Hermione came into her life.

It was the Saturday before Memorial Day and three clerks had called in sick, so there was only one checkout open. The line at Peterson's Market snaked through the produce area and back past meats. Hermione, with her six large watermelons, stood directly in front of Lillian.

Were it not for the fact that the line moved slower than molasses Lillian would have said nothing, but after fifteen minutes of standing in one spot curiosity got the best of her.

"What are you going to do with all that watermelon?" she asked.

Hermione chuckled. "I's supposed to bring dessert to the party, and there ain't nothing sweeter than summer watermelon."

"That's the God's honest truth," Lillian replied.

"They got plenty more back there," Hermione said. "If you want to go grab yourself one, I'll save you a place in line."

Lillian gave a sorrowful sigh and explained that she'd been alone since Walter passed on, and as much as she loved watermelon a whole one would surely rot before she got around to finishing it.

Hermione peered into Lillian's basket and spied the four cans of Chef Boyardee spaghetti and a single can of Spam.

"You planning to eat that stuff?" she asked.

Lillian nodded.

Hermione raised an eyebrow. "Woman like you ought to know there ain't a peanut's worth of nutrition in that mush."

"Well, it's not easy when you're cooking for one," Lillian replied defensively.

"That ain't even cooking. That's just heating up!"

Hermione pushed the pitiful looking basket to the side and hooked her arm through Lillian's.

"You is coming with me," she said. "It's time you learned what good eatin' is."

That was Lillian's introduction to Hermione Bushweiler and Baylor Towers.

Two weeks later she put her house on the market, and within the month she'd moved into a one-bedroom apartment two floors up from Hermione.

When she walked out of her house for the last time she finally said goodbye to Walter. She carried the good memories with her and left the bad ones behind.

Not once has she regretted the move.

STUDYING THE DAZED LOOK ON Ophelia's face, Lillian asks again, "You sure you don't want me to call for a doctor?"

Ophelia shakes her head. "I'll be alright. I just need to do some thinking."

Lillian reaches over and hugs Ophelia. "I'm here if you need me." She pulls the divider to a partially open position. It is enough to afford Ophelia privacy while still allowing Lillian to keep an eye on her.

THAT MORNING OPHELIA BARELY PICKS at her breakfast, and when Lillian's friends come to play pinochle she declines an invitation to join them.

"I'm afraid I wouldn't be much fun today," she says. "I've got worrisome things on my mind."

"Playing pinochle is a good way to forget your worries," Pauline suggests.

"Not today," Ophelia repeats.

She leans back into the pillow and closes her eyes. Although she is not part of the game, Ophelia listens to every word that is said. Remaining on the sideline, she can hear the sound of friendship. Not the type of friendship she has with Annie but a partnership of equals. A back-and-forth good-natured chiding that has fondness squeezed between the barbs.

"You're the worst pinochle player ever," Lillian tells Sam.

He laughs. "Yeah, but that's because you cheat. I saw you palm that card!"

"Why, I never..."

Pauline gives a deep hearty laugh.

The sound of such a laugh brings back memories Ophelia had perhaps forgotten. She allows her thoughts to slide back to the countless evenings she and Edward shared with friends: dinner parties, croquet on the lawn, Sunday picnic lunches.

She recalls the time ten friends crowded into Edward's new convertible and drove all the way into Richmond just to see the new Marilyn Monroe movie. Ophelia had laughed until her sides ached, and, oh, what fun they had. Funny that after all the years she is just now remembering these things.

FOUR HANDS HAVE BEEN PLAYED when Ophelia calls out, "On second thought I will join you."

"Great," Sam says, "I'll grab a chair for you."

Ophelia climbs out of bed and pushes the divider curtain open. "I can't let you have all the fun without me."

Pauline deals the cards and a new game begins.

WHEN THE AID COMES WITH lunch trays for Ophelia and Lillian, they set aside the cards. Pauline and Sadie have brought their own lunch in a brown bag. Sam has no bag, so the others share. He eats half of Pauline's sandwich, Sadie's crackers, Ophelia's pudding and the bowl of orange slices on Lillian's tray.

During lunch Ophelia asks the question picking at her mind.

"Such wonderful friendships," she says. "How did you all meet?"

"Baylor Towers," they reply in unison.

"What's Baylor Towers?"

"A senior residence," Lillian replies. "We all have apartments in the building."

"Yeah," Sam adds, "and the good thing is no kids! Dogs, cats, fish, even monkeys are okay, but no kids."

Throughout the remainder of lunch they talk of the parties and games of Baylor.

"Poker night," Sam says. "That's my favorite."

"Fiddlesticks," Pauline counters. "That doesn't hold a candle to the Valentine's Day dance. All those heart decorations and streamers…"

When they have finished eating and the trays are taken away, Ophelia is not ready for this conversation to end. She pulls out the box of chocolates Oliver has sent her and sets it on the table with a smile.

"I thought we could all use a bit of sweetness."

Sam eyes the box. "Are there caramels in here? I can't eat caramels."

"Well, I can," Lillian says and plucks a big fat chocolate from the center of the box.

It is almost three-thirty when they finally resume their game. Ophelia, now quite invigorated, wins both rounds. She is ready for a third game when Tyrone shows up with the wheelchair and carts her off to therapy.

"Oh, darn," she says. "I hate to leave when I'm winning,"

"You ain't moving in here permanently," Tyrone laughs. "You is here for the exercise what gets people better." His laughter is contagious.

"Yeah," Sam says. "Get well enough to come on over to Baylor and be my poker partner. I been having a bad streak and I could use..."

The remainder of what he says is lost when Tyrone wheels Ophelia from the room.

OPHELIA

For the first time in all these years I'm thinking of moving away from Memory House. I never thought I'd consider such a thing, but here I am saying it.

Last night after everybody went home Lil and I sat up talking. She told me something I wouldn't have in a million years suspected. She said she had awful dreams after Walter died.

I look at Lil and see a woman tough as nails, but the truth is she's not that way at all. She acts gruff and matter-of-fact, but once you see past all that huffing and puffing she's got heartaches the same as me.

She said when her Walter died, she went through the exact same misery I had when I lost Edward. The thing that saved her was moving out of that house. She claims memories are something you need to pass on to young people. According to Lil, weighing yourself down with a truckload of memories will just hold you back from moving on and enjoying the rest of your years.

I never told Annie this, but I was figuring to leave her Memory House. She loves it there, and I've got no one else. In my heart I'm certain as certain can be that Edward brought that girl to my door. It's just like him to do such a thing. When he was alive, he always took good care of me and I think he's still doing it.

Fred Worthington said the house is too old to be worth much, but the property is valuable. He claims he could sell it in less than a minute. A smart buyer would knock the place down and put in a sprawling single-story ranch, he said. All the time he was talking I was thinking, Over my dead body.

That's why I had to find somebody before my time came, somebody who could take over the memories and appreciate the place. It would break my heart to see a house with so much happiness in it sold to a perfect stranger.

Fred's a lawyer, which explains why he thinks that way. Everybody knows lawyers don't have a heart. Most lawyers anyway. Ethan Allen and Oliver are exceptions, but that's probably why they changed from lawyering to being judges.

Being a judge, now that's a respectable profession.

I'M NOT ONE HUNDRED PERCENT *sure of what I'm going to do, but I'm keeping an open mind. I'm hoping Edward will come visit me soon and I can talk to him about it.*

MAX'S VISITS

In the days that follow, Max makes three different visits to Memory House. The first time it is to study the bookcases in the loft. She pokes around the dividing walls for several minutes then frowns. It is as she feared. The bookcase is built as a single unit and impossible to move intact.

Trying to sound optimistic she says, "We can explore other options."

Annie asks what those options are.

Pinching her brows together, Max closes her eyes and runs her hand along the end of the bookcase. It is almost a full minute before her eyes pop open and she speaks.

"The most cost efficient way would be to match the wood and duplicate the construction, but..."

"But what?" Annie asks.

"There are a lot of memories in this wood," Max says. "If we built a new bookcase it will look the same, but it won't have the memories."

"You can feel the memories?"

Max nods, then explains the alternative would be to take the bookcase apart shelf by shelf and reassemble it in the new room.

"The problem is that would be a lot more expensive."

"How much more?"

Max feels along the back edge of several shelves then gives another frown. "Glued tight," she says. "Taking it apart is going to be slow and labor intensive."

"So how much?" Annie asks.

"I'm better at getting the feel of a place than doing numbers off the top of my head, but I'd guess three to five thousand."

Annie gives a low whistle.

"You don't have to decide now," Max says. "I'll pencil in both options on the drawing and give you estimates."

AS THEY ARE DESCENDING THE STAIRS Annie asks if Max has time for a cup of tea.

"Absolutely," she answers.

A pot of lemon balm tea already sits on the back of the stove. Today Annie has brewed a calming blend. When she works in the apothecary she wants her mind to be relaxed and open to all thoughts. She hopes one day she will discover the magic of Ophelia's special potpourri.

She adds a teaspoon of honey to each cup then fills a plate with ginger cookies and carries the tray to the back porch. Much the same as she did with Ophelia, Annie and Max sit across from one another in the wicker chairs.

The day is warm, but here it is comfortable. The swans glide across the pond, and a soft breeze ripples the water. Max catches the scent of the flower garden.

"This is such a beautiful spot," she says. "No wonder Ophelia loves it."

"It's this house," Annie replies. "It has a magic of its own."

Max nods agreement then talks about her year in Paris.

"The peacefulness here is like what I found at Tuileries

Gardens," she says. "No pond, but a lovely fountain." Her face takes on a look of remembering. "Julian and I spent countless afternoons there."

Annie's mouth curls into a smile. She can feel a certain fondness attached to the name. "Was this Julien someone special?"

"For a while," Max says. "But once I came home..." Her words trail off.

Although she already surmises the answer, Annie says, "He didn't come to visit?"

Max shakes her head sadly. "Not even an email." She pushes thoughts of Julian from her head and says, "But I'm totally over him now."

Annie doubts this is true but accepts the answer and switches back to talking about the project.

"I'm super anxious to introduce you to Ophelia," she says. "When do you think the drawings will be ready?"

Max fingers her chin thoughtfully. "Late next week?" She hooks a question mark onto the end of her answer, hoping for an approval.

"Perfect," Annie says.

Ophelia has another two weeks at the rehab center; then she will be coming home. For the evening of her return, they will plan a special dinner party. That same evening they will introduce Max and unveil the drawing for the new room.

TWO DAYS LATER MAX RETURNS. This time she hauls a twelve-foot ladder to the loft so she can get the exact dimensions of the skylight.

"Brace this at the bottom, and make sure it doesn't tilt," she tells Annie, then scoots up the ladder and stretches her folding yardstick in one direction and the other.

This task takes less than a half-hour, but again Max stays for tea and doesn't leave until Oliver returns from the courthouse.

When Annie hears him call out that he's home, she can scarcely believe how the time has flown. That evening instead of visiting Ophelia, she telephones.

"I'm sorry," she says. "I'd planned to come for a visit, but the afternoon got away from me."

Ophelia's voice is breezy and light. There is no sound of disappointment. "That's okay," she says. "I'm kind of busy anyway."

"Busy? Doing what?"

Ophelia giggles. "Beating Sam's butt at pinochle."

They talk for less than a minute; then Ophelia says she's got to go. Annie senses she is anxious to get back to the game.

"I'll be there Friday afternoon for sure," she says and hangs up.

AS IT TURNS OUT, MAX is back again on Friday. This time she comes carrying a chilled bottle of champagne.

"Celebration time," she says and holds out the bottle.

Annie laughs. "What exactly are we celebrating?"

"Thanks to that channeling tea you made for me, I've got two new clients."

"How wonderful!" Annie exclaims. "But I really don't think it was the tea. It's probably more because—"

Max shakes her head. "It's the tea. I'm certain of it." Her smile is stretched the full width of her face when she asks if Annie has time for a glass of champagne.

"Since you're responsible for my good fortune," she says, "I thought we could celebrate together."

"Of course," Annie replies.

True, she has planned to visit Ophelia. But over the weeks Max has also become a friend, and Annie wants to share this moment of happiness. A flicker of guilt tickles the back of Annie's mind, but she pushes it away.

I'll call Ophelia this evening, she tells herself. *Then tomorrow I'll spend the entire afternoon with her.* This is enough to appease her conscience.

Max pops open the bottle of champagne, and Annie carries a small basket of salted zucchini chips to the back porch. They settle into the chairs, and in less than a heartbeat they are involved in a conversation that has the sound of lifelong friends.

The Decision

On Friday Baylor Towers is hosting a party, so none of the pinochle players visit. Lillian and Ophelia are alone in the room when Annie calls to say she won't be able to make it.

"Tomorrow will be fine," Ophelia says, but Lillian hears the disappointment in her voice.

Waiting until the receiver is back in its cradle, Lillian glances over with a raised eyebrow. "That's the third time this week."

"I can count," Ophelia replies, her words rather testy.

Lillian slides a slip of paper into the book she's reading and closes the cover. "I hate to say I told you so, but—"

"Then don't say it," Ophelia cuts in. "I understand why Annie's busy. She's taking care of the apothecary and—"

Without allowing Ophelia to finish the thought, Lillian says, "She's a young woman who wants to spend some time alone with her new husband." A second later she adds, "Which is perfectly normal."

Ophelia lets this thought settle in her head and says nothing. Several minutes pass before she sheepishly admits there's a possibility that Lillian is right.

"After our talk a few nights ago, I've been giving some serious consideration to moving into a place like Baylor Towers," she says.

"Why not Baylor Towers itself?" Lillian asks. Without waiting for an answer she enumerates the countless reasons for choosing Baylor Towers, not the least of which is the dozen or more friends who live there.

"I just might do that," Ophelia says with a smile. "Of course, first I'd have to visit the place and make certain I like it."

"Oh, you'll like it." Lillian gives a grin of satisfaction. "I'm certain of that." She climbs from her bed, comes around and sits in the chair beside Ophelia. "There's never a dull moment. Why, when they have the Saint Patrick's Day party..."

They talk late into the evening and when Ophelia's eyes finally begin to flutter, Lillian sashays back to her own bed. She waits until she hears the soft sounds of Ophelia's sleep and then dials Pauline's number.

"Okay, this is what we have to do..." She whispers the plan, and Pauline is in full agreement.

THE NEXT MORNING BEFORE THE breakfast trays have been delivered, Sam walks in.

"I was up early," he says, "so I thought I'd stop by for a visit." By some odd circumstance, he's carrying a photo album filled with snapshots of Baylor Towers.

"I thought maybe you'd like to see this." He plops down alongside Ophelia and begins to flip through the pages.

"This is the new pool table," he explains. "And this one's the card room. Poker every Friday night." He segues into a tale of how he's lost for the past eight years and could use a card-smart partner, then looks square into Ophelia's eye.

"I'm thinking you'd fit the bill perfectly."

She laughs. "I doubt that. The only game I know is pinochle and maybe a smidgen of bridge."

"But you're a natural," Sam says. "I can tell."

Before he has finished showing his album, Pauline arrives. She's got pictures of pets: dogs, cats and even a small monkey. She shoves the photo of a sad-eyed beagle in front of Ophelia and says, "This is Buster; he belongs to Tess Abrams. You're going to love Tess, she's a barrel of laughs."

"But I haven't actually decided—"

"And this is Mildred's poodle. Smartest dog I've ever seen. Mildred tells her to go get the bunny toy, and Poopsie digs through her basket until she finds that stuffed rabbit."

One by one Pauline goes through the photos describing both the pet and the owner. When she has exhausted her supply of photos, she apologizes for not having a shot of Calvin's aquarium but adds that it's a beauty.

After Pauline, Mildred comes with pictures of both her apartment and Poopsie. Several others follow her. That afternoon by the time Annie and Oliver arrive Ophelia has seen photos of everything, including the empty one-bedroom with a terrace that overlooks the gardens. She has all but made up her mind, yet she says nothing. It is too early. There are arrangements to be made. Legalities to be addressed.

Oliver kisses Ophelia on the cheek and hands her a second box of chocolates. "You're looking well," he says.

Ophelia does look good. She is rested and happy. For the first time in more years than she can remember, she has made a decision without consulting the stars.

As they move into an easy conversation, Ophelia notices how Oliver tugs Annie close to his side and how she in turn blushes at his touch. They are happy, quite possibly as happy as she was with Edward.

Watching them together, a thought comes to her.

"You two should move into the loft," she says. "The doctor said no stairs, so I won't be using it."

Annie shakes her head. "We couldn't. Edward built that room for you. It's a place where—"

Ophelia stops her. "Edward's gone. But he intended the room to be a place for lovers. I think he'd be pleased to know I've passed it on to someone I love."

Annie notices something different. It's a strange new level of acceptance in Ophelia's voice. This is the first time she's spoken of Edward as if he is actually gone, actually dead.

She lifts Ophelia's hand into hers. A worried expression knits her brows.

"Are you okay?" she asks. "The doctor hasn't said something we should know about, has he?"

"I'm fine," Ophelia says. "Better than ever. Being here has actually been good for me."

"Well, don't get too comfortable," Oliver warns. "In less than two weeks, you'll be coming home."

When he says this Ophelia forces a smile, but Annie catches the pinched expression on her face.

"You're sure you're okay?" she asks again.

They stay until the dinner trays come, and then Ophelia chases them out.

"I need my rest," she says.

AS SOON AS THEIR FOOTSTEPS DISAPPEAR down the hallway, Ophelia picks up the telephone and dials Fred Worthington's number. It's Saturday and the probability is he won't be in his office, but she'll leave a message and say it's a matter of urgency.

She is set to talk to the machine, but he picks up on the third ring.

"Worthington," he says.

"Is that you, Fred?"

"Yes," he answers. "Who's this?"

"Ophelia." She waits for a response, but there is none. "Ophelia Browne," she clarifies. "Edward Browne's wife."

"Well, I'll be damned," he says with a hearty laugh. "I haven't heard from you in a dog's age. Where've you been keeping yourself?"

"In the same place as always," she answers. "Except for the past few weeks. I'm not at Memory House; now I'm at the Kipling Rehabilitation Center."

"What's wrong?" he asks.

"Nothing," she replies. "Everything is fine, but I need to speak with you about a business matter."

"So," Fred says, "you're finally going to sell the house, huh?"

"No," Ophelia answers. "I'm going to give it away."

CHANGES

On Monday morning Fred arrives with a stack of documents for Ophelia to sign. Giving away the house turns out to be not quite as easy as she'd anticipated. Before the property can be transferred Fred claims there are issues of tax escrow, title search and legality of sale to be addressed. He says to establish a bona fide transaction, Annie needs to pay Ophelia at least $100.

"Now if you were dead, that wouldn't be necessary. She could receive it as part of your estate."

"I'm not dead!" Ophelia snaps.

After three trips back and forth to the Kipling Center, Fred shows up Thursday afternoon with the last of the paperwork. He hands Ophelia an overstuffed folder and says, "This is it. Once Annie signs these papers, the house is hers."

Ophelia beams. "Thank you."

"Don't thank me," Fred replies sharply. "I've already told you this goes against my better judgment. You could have gotten a good price for that property—"

"This is what makes me happy," Ophelia replies. "And that's enough for me."

"Makes you happy?" Fred shakes his head morosely. "What about Edward? I doubt he'd approve of you giving away something he worked hard to—"

Ophelia interrupts. "You're wrong. He approves wholeheartedly."

She knows this for a fact, because once her decision was made Edward came to her in a dream. A dream so sweet it lingers still.

ANNIE VISITS THE KIPLING CENTER on Tuesday afternoon, but for the remainder of the week she is busy tending the garden and running the apothecary. She is also readying the house for Ophelia's return.

Although Max has already applied for a building permit, the new room will not be completed for several months. Until then, Ophelia will sleep in the room across the hall from Oliver and Annie.

It is only for a short while, but Annie wants Ophelia to be happy in the room. She has decorated it with a new comforter and new draperies. Next to the bed she has added a small table with dried flowers and a basket of the jasmine potpourri she created. It is not nearly as pungent as Ophelia's but seems as though it is capable of sometimes changing aromas.

Annie first suspects this on Wednesday when Max delivers the final drawings. After they've pored over every last detail of the plan, she shows Max the bedroom Ophelia will use until the construction is complete. The moment they walk in, she catches the scent of chocolate.

Although Annie is hard pressed to say what prompts her to ask, she turns to Max and says, "Would you like a cup of hot chocolate?"

Max registers a look of surprise. "Is it that obvious?"

"No, but when we came in here I thought I smelled—"

"I smelled it too," Max says. "Did you move the potpourri from the hallway?"

Annie smiles and shakes her head. "No, this is one I mixed."

"Wow," Max laughs. "You've definitely got the power."

THAT AFTERNOON THEY SIT ON the screened porch and have hot chocolate with sugar cookies. Again they talk of Max's year in Paris. She tells of the bistros where she and Julian sipped chocolate so sweet it lingered on her tongue for hours and of romantic walks along the Seine.

Max smiles with the sweetness of such a thought. "They say the Seine is the river of love."

She hesitates a moment then tells of that last week when Julian bought a yellow lock symbolic of their love.

"He took me to a bridge that crosses the Seine and clipped the lock onto the wire fence. I'll never forget how he kissed me then hurled that key into the river."

She gives a long sigh thick with the memory. "It meant as lovers we were forever locked to one another, but..."

"Did you ever try emailing him?" Annie asks.

Max gives a saddened shake of her head. "When I didn't hear from him I figured it was a fling and he was ready to move on."

"It's never too late to try."

A smile appears on Max's face. "That was three years ago. By now he's probably married and got a toddler walking around."

Although Max does not say this, the thought of reaching out to Julian has crossed her mind countless times. But she has never mustered up the courage to do so. In her mind the memory left undisturbed retains its sweetness. Pried open to reveal the truth, it could sour and turn rancid. A good memory is better than nothing.

She moves back to talk of Ophelia's return. "So what's the plan?"

Annie tells of how she is arranging a dinner party for the day of Ophelia's return.

"Small," she says, "but fancy. Ophelia has no family, so it will be just the four of us. Me, Oliver, Ophelia and, of course, you."

"I'll bring champagne," Max volunteers.

Annie nods. It is an added touch of festivity she hadn't thought of.

THE WEEK FLIES BY, AND it is Saturday before Annie has a chance to visit the Kipling Center. When she walks into the room, the first thing she notices is that the bed next to Ophelia is empty.

"Where's Lillian?" she asks.

"She was discharged this morning," Ophelia replies sadly.

Annie can tell Ophelia's been crying. "Just because she went home doesn't mean you can't remain friends."

"I know," Ophelia replies. "But it was so nice having her here beside me." She tells the story Lillian has told her, the one about why she went to live at Baylor Towers. She hopes Annie will catch hold of the message behind the story, but she doesn't.

"I guess being all alone like that is why Lillian needed to find a place where she had friends. Luckily you don't have that problem," Annie says. "You have me."

Before Ophelia can move into what she hopes to say, Annie segues into how she's redecorated the bedroom across the hall.

"The comforter is covered with bright pink cabbage roses," she says. "I think you'll love it."

"I'm sure I will," Ophelia says, suppressing a sigh.

Determined to fill the emptiness left by Lillian, Annie chatters about all the things they will do once Ophelia comes home.

"It's less than a week now," she says cheerfully.

AT THREE O'CLOCK SAM AND Pauline come for a visit. Ophelia's face brightens the moment they come through the door, and Annie notices this.

Sam comes to the side of the bed, plants a kiss on Ophelia's cheek and says, "Lil couldn't make it today, but she'll be here tomorrow." He gives a toothy grin and adds, "She gave us the good news that you're—"

Ophelia senses what he is about to say and moves to stop him. In a voice that's barely a shade lower than yelling, she says, "You mean the good news that I'm going home next Friday?"

The remainder of Sam's words is buried beneath Ophelia's voice.

Before he can get back to the subject, Ophelia grabs the water pitcher and hands it to Annie. "Would you mind getting some fresh ice water from down the hall?"

"Of course not." Annie takes the pitcher and trots out.

As soon as she is gone from the room Ophelia whispers loudly, "I haven't told her yet!"

Pauline and Sam both give an understanding nod.

After she returns with the water Annie stays for another hour. She remains in the background as she watches Ophelia laughing and enjoying the company of her newfound friends. Seeing her so happy gives Annie an idea, one she is surprised she hasn't thought of sooner.

Before leaving, she tugs Pauline into the hallway and whispers, "Next Friday we're having a welcome home dinner party for Ophelia, and we'd love to have you, Sam and Lillian join us." She hands Pauline a scribbled note with the address.

"Um, I'm not sure..." Pauline stutters.

"If it's transportation, I can have Oliver pick you up and drive you home."

"That's not a problem," Pauline says. "Baylor Towers has a car service for us, but—"

"Oh, please come," Annie begs. "It would mean so much to Ophelia."

Pauline reluctantly says she will have to first check with Sam and Lillian.

"Can I call you?" she asks.

Annie nods at the note. "My cell phone number is right there on the bottom." She turns to leave then looks back and adds, "But not a word to Ophelia; the party is going to be a surprise."

As Annie disappears down the hall, Pauline shakes her head ruefully. Normally no one likes a party better than Pauline, but she can already smell trouble in the air.

ANNIE

It's funny how things work out. This afternoon when I went to visit Ophelia she looked kind of gloomy. With Lillian gone and the other bed empty, it was pretty understandable. I thought maybe it would cheer her up if I told her about all the fun we'd have when she came home. It didn't. But when her friends came in, she started looking a whole lot happier.

Watching her laugh at those silly jokes of Sam's I saw a different Ophelia. Not better or worse, just different. With me she's the teacher and I'm the student. Even with all the wonderful times we've had together, I never once saw her laugh the way she did with Sam and Pauline.

That made me realize how selfish I've been. No matter how old somebody gets, they still need friends. Not someone to watch over and protect the way Ophelia does me, but someone who's an equal. Somebody who makes you laugh the way Sam makes Ophelia laugh.

I guess the truth is no matter how much Ophelia and I love one another, it's not the same as having your own friends.

I've got Oliver and Max and Giselle, but up until now the only really close person Ophelia had was me. I know she says she's got Edward, but a memory isn't the same as having a person there to sit down and share a cup of coffee.

I hope Sam, Pauline and Lillian all come to Ophelia's welcome home party. I can't think of anything that would make her happier—except maybe seeing the drawing for the new room.

On the way home I made a decision. Once a week I'm going to drive Ophelia into town so she can visit her friends at Baylor Towers. And if she wants, I'll do it more than once a week.

I can hardly wait to see the smile on her face when she finds out she's getting a room exactly like the loft and going into town to see her friends every single week.

COMING HOME

Two days later Ophelia is told she is getting a new roommate. She hopes for someone like Lillian, but Gertrude Kaminski turns out to be a woman with her eyebrows pinched together and her mouth puckered into a pout.

Thinking Gertrude most likely feels as lost as she did the first day, Ophelia does what Lillian would have done. She climbs from her bed, thumps her way past the half-closed divider curtain and asks, "Would you like this curtain pushed open?"

"Unh-uh," Gertrude says and shakes her head.

"I thought maybe we could chat. Get to know one another."

"No thanks," Gertrude says and turns her face to the wall.

Before Ophelia gets back to her side of the room, Gertrude's daughter comes running in. She is red-faced and winded.

"Sorry, Mama," she says. "I hurried much as I could, but the gift shop—"

"Phoebe." Gertrude's mouth slides into a sneer. "Did you or did you not get me my spearmint gum?"

"I didn't, Mama, but the reason—"

Gertrude gives a loud huff. "I ask for one little thing, and you can't do it?"

"I tried, Mama, but—"

"Hush up those excuses, and close that curtain. I don't like strangers poking their nose in my business."

As Phoebe closes the divider curtain she smiles at Ophelia and shrugs.

FOR THE REMAINDER OF THE day, the only time Ophelia sees Gertrude is when she passes by the inside bed on her way to the bathroom or when she goes to the sunroom to watch the *Ellen Degeneres Show*. Although she doesn't see much of the woman, she hears everything.

BEFORE THE FIRST DAY IS out Phoebe has told her mama if she doesn't stop nagging her about every little thing, she's gonna find herself with no place to live.

"That would be just like you to do such a thing to your poor old mama," Gertrude replies. "After all the years I did without just so you could have—"

"You never did without anything, Mama. You was so demanding of Daddy he run off and left you. Now you're doing it to me." Phoebe makes a noise that is somewhere between a moan and a cry of anguish.

"If you had your way, you'd run poor Harold off the way you did Daddy," she says. "Then you'd have me waiting on you hand and foot!"

"You should've never married Harold," Gertrude says. "He's a worthless piece of—"

"Just shut up, Mama! Shut up, or I swear I'll walk out of here and never come back!"

When Lillian and Sam come to visit the next afternoon, Ophelia suggests they go down to the sunroom.

"No need," Lillian says. "We'll just invite your roomie to play."

Before Ophelia can whisper a background of what's been happening, Lillian pulls back the divider curtain and asks Gertrude if she'd like to join in a game of pinochle.

"No, I don't! Playing cards is a heathen's way of shaking hands with the devil!"

Lillian gives her a look of disbelief. "It's pinochle!"

"Shut that curtain before I call the nurse and have you thrown outta here for disturbing the patients."

"Suit yourself, you old crab ass," Lillian says.

Sam gathers the cards, and they head for the sunroom.

As they walk down the hall, Lillian says, "Good grief, that woman is awful."

"Her daughter is almost as bad," Ophelia replies. "You ought to hear the way they go at it tooth and nail."

"I'll bet they live together," Lillian says.

Ophelia nods. "I think so."

"That's exactly why I didn't go live with my Chrissie," Lillian says. "I love her to pieces, and she loves me too, but people can get on each other's nerves and before you know it love turns as sour as month old milk."

"That's true enough," Sam agrees.

While Ophelia says nothing more about this, in her mind it confirms that she has made the right decision. Hopefully Annie will agree.

ON FRIDAY MORNING SHE IS scheduled to go home, and Ophelia is ready to leave before the breakfast trays are served. She has had more than enough of Phoebe and Gertrude's squabbling. It is barely nine o'clock, but her bag is packed.

She is dressed and sitting in the chair when Annie arrives.

Seeing this, Annie smiles. She too is glad Ophelia is coming home. It will be a responsibility caring for her but a responsibility Annie is happy to have.

After the last of the paperwork is signed the nurse wheels Ophelia to the front exit, and they wait for Annie to bring the car around. When she pulls up, Annie jumps from the car and comes around to assist Ophelia. Before there is a moment to object, she lifts Ophelia's legs into the car and checks to see that all fingers and toes are clear of the door.

"You don't have a thing to worry about," she says. "I'm going to take good care of you."

"I don't need caring for," Ophelia replies. "I'm perfectly capable of taking care of myself. I could have easily as not walked to the car."

Annie rolls past Ophelia's words and tells how everything has been readied for her return.

"I've clipped a bouquet of fresh peonies for your room," she says. "I know how you love those."

"You needn't have."

"It was no bother."

Annie watches the road as she drives and doesn't see the perplexed expression on Ophelia's face.

"And wait until you hear what we're having for dinner," she continues. "Oliver bought a gas grill for the backyard, and tonight he's barbequing steaks. After having hospital food for so long, I bet you'll really enjoy a nice juicy steak."

"Actually the food at Kipling was pretty good. Tasty, but nice and light."

WHEN THEY ARRIVE AT MEMORY House, Ophelia feels the weight of remembering heavy in her heart. She aches to climb the stairs and again be in the loft. For a moment she pauses at the foot of the staircase, remembering the first time she danced up the stairs with Edward trailing behind her. Oh, how they'd laughed with delight. Three times they raced up and down the new staircase; then, exhausted, they fell upon the bed, still laughing at the foolishness of such play.

Ophelia moves on, past the parlor with its puffy chintz sofa and chiming clock, past the dining room with its mahogany table and into the back bedroom. The room has a fresh new look. She turns to Annie.

"It looks lovely."

Annie asks if Ophelia is tired. "Would you prefer to take a nap, or shall I make lunch and we'll sit on the back porch?"

Ophelia opts for lunch on the porch. She hopes that a few quiet moments together will enable her to say what she has to say.

Annie hurries into the kitchen, and Ophelia follows close behind.

"I'll fix a salad," Ophelia says and pulls open the refrigerator door.

"Oh, no, you don't," Annie says and pushes the door closed. "You're not going to lift a finger. Just sit down and relax; I'm here to take care of you." With her arm around Ophelia's shoulder, she eases her over to the kitchen chair.

"But I want to help," Ophelia argues.

This is true. She has spent her life moving about the kitchen as Annie is now doing, and it saddens her to step aside. It makes her feel older than her ninety years. Helpless almost.

"Dandelion or peppermint tea?" Annie asks.

"Dandelion," Ophelia answers wearily. She wants to fill the diffuser herself, but she is no match for the formidable force of Annie's love.

ONCE THEY ARE SETTLED ON the porch, they talk of all that has happened in the time she has been gone.

"I've met a new friend," Annie says. "Max. She's an architect."

"I'm enjoying some new friends also," Ophelia replies. "They all live at Baylor Towers, an apartment building specially designed for seniors. The thing about living at Baylor is—"

"I met your new friends at the rehab center," Annie says. "They're lovely people. In fact I've invited Lillian, Sam and Pauline to your welcome home dinner."

"Welcome home dinner?"

Annie nods. "I was saving it as a surprise, but then I thought you might want to get dressed up since it's going to be a party."

"When you invited them here, did they say anything?" Ophelia asks cautiously.

"If you mean did they thank me for inviting them," Annie says, smiling, "they most certainly did. Lillian said she wouldn't miss it for the world."

"Did she tell you anything about Baylor Towers?"

"No," Annie replies, "but we didn't talk that long. I'm sure we'll have more time to talk tonight."

Ophelia had planned to tell Annie of her surprise at dinner, but this turn of events changes things. Debating about whether she should say something now or wait until tomorrow, she lifts her glass and drains the last of the iced tea.

"Now that you're home," Annie says, "you should stay in touch with your friends. Maybe once or twice a week we could go into town and stop by for a visit."

This is the opening Ophelia has been looking for.

"I was thinking I'd like to be with them more often," she says.

"No problem," Annie replies. "We can go as often as you like." Seconds later she is off to the kitchen to refill their glasses.

Before Annie returns the front door clicks open, and Oliver calls out saying he is home. Ophelia gives a saddened sigh; what she has to say will have to wait until tomorrow.

OPHELIA

It's devilish hard to say something you know is going to hurt somebody you love, and I love Annie as much as I'd love a child borne of my body. It won't be easy to flat out say it's time for both of us to start living our own life. But I believe it's the right thing to do, and I'm praying God will give me the strength to stay firm.

Sometimes I'm all fired sure I'm doing the right thing; then other times I start doubting myself. When that happens, I think back on how it was with Phoebe and her mama. Every mama loves her baby, and I'm sure there was a time when Gertrude loved her daughter. But it seems living together killed that love. I never met Phoebe's husband, but I can guarantee you he's not a happy man. How can he be with that kind of friction going on day in and day out?

Mind you, I'm not comparing Annie to Phoebe. Annie has a kind heart. I can't in my wildest dreams imagine she'd ever talk to me the way Phoebe talked to her mama. But that doesn't change the reality of things.

The reality is young people need to be alone together. They need time to discover one another, find their hopes and dreams, and plan for a future. In a few years babies will come along, and it will be too late for these things. They'll move on to being a family, and their thoughts will be about doing what's best for their babies.

That's not a bad thing. It's simply the way life happens. But years from now when those responsibilities come at them like a steamroller, they'll think back on these early days. That's when they'll be glad they had this time to lie in the grass and do nothing but enjoy the closeness of each other. The memory of such sweetness is what carries a person through the hard years.

I'm hoping Oliver will understand the wisdom of what I'm saying, even if Annie doesn't. Annie loves me, and love sometimes gets in the way of seeing things clearly.

I know she won't be happy when I first tell her, but time will change that. Once she settles into a life of her own, she'll understand the truth of what I've been saying. Until then, Annie's got a good man by her side. He'll take care of her.

A Sad Surprise

When the guests arrive Ophelia is wearing the blue silk dress she saves for special occasions. She is ready and waiting when the doorbell rings.

"I'll get it," she says and scurries off.

As she suspects, it is Lillian. Sam and Pauline are just steps behind. In the few seconds she has before Annie comes to welcome them, Ophelia whispers a warning that she has not yet told anyone of her plan.

Lillian gives a knowing wink.

Max arrives not long after Ophelia's friends, and the others happen along minutes later. Once they are all together, Annie carries in a tray with seven glasses of champagne. She hands one to each guest, gives one to Oliver and Ophelia and keeps one for herself.

"Tonight is a very special occasion," she says. "We are welcoming Ophelia home. She has been sorely missed around here."

"And she's gonna be missed a whole lot more," Sam says.

Lillian slides her hand behind his back and gives him a good hard pinch.

"What Sam means to say," she says, "is that we are all going to miss the good times and pinochle games we had at Kipling."

"That's not what I meant," Sam says.

Lillian pinches him a second time.

"Ouch!" he yells. "That hurt."

Lillian leans in and brushes her napkin across the front of Sam's shirt as if she has splashed a bit of champagne on him.

"I'm so sorry," she says loudly. Beneath her breath she whispers, "It's going to hurt a whole lot more if you don't keep quiet."

"Okay, that's what I meant," Sam says. "I'll miss the pinochle games."

AFTER TWO MORE ROUNDS OF champagne and a steak that Sam declares "the best he's ever tasted," Annie feels the time is right for her surprise. She raps the blade of her knife against the edge of the plate and everyone turns.

"You've all met my friend Max," she says, "but I haven't yet told you the reason she is here. Max is an architect, and she has designed something very special as a welcome home gift for Ophelia."

She gives a subtle nod and Oliver leaves the room. He comes back carrying an easel and what appears to be a large painting. He sets it in a spot where everyone can easily see.

He nods back and Annie continues. "As you know, because of her heart attack Ophelia can no longer climb the stairs. We've looked into the possibility of a lift chair, but unfortunately the staircase is too narrow.

She turns toward Oliver with a look of adoration. "So my wonderful husband came up with this alternative."

Just as they've planned, Annie waves her hand and he unveils the drawing of the lookalike room.

Ophelia views it with a quizzical eye. "A picture of the loft?"

"Not a picture," Oliver says. "It's an architectural rendering of your new room in the wing."

Ophelia squints at the drawing then looks up at Oliver. "What wing?"

"The one we're planning to build," he says proudly. "Annie told me how much the loft means to you, so we thought it would be nice to recreate it right here on the ground floor. By adding this room you'll be able to enjoy the things you love without having to climb stairs."

"And," Max adds, "the bookcases from the loft will be moved to the new room, so you'll still have all those wonderful memories."

Ophelia's face falls. "Lord have mercy," she says through a gasp and clutches her hand to her chest.

Annie jumps from her seat and dashes to Ophelia's side. "Is it your heart?"

Ophelia shakes her head but says nothing. She just sits there looking like the ceiling has fallen on her head.

When Oliver asks if he should call for the doctor, she again shakes her head.

"It's a beautiful plan," she finally says. Her words come slowly with long pauses between them. "I am blessed to have the two of you care so much about my happiness, but I have also planned a surprise."

Ophelia pushes back from the table, goes to the bedroom and returns with a fat envelope. She hands it to Annie.

"I don't want to change this house," she says. "I want to forever remember it exactly as it is."

"This was only a suggestion," Oliver says. "We don't have to—"

Ophelia holds up the palm of her hand. "It was a beautiful thought, more than I could possibly ask for. But there comes a time when people need to live their own life." She smiles at Annie and suggests she open the envelope.

Annie does as she is told then looks up with that same type of quizzical expression. "I don't get it. What does this mean?"

"Memory House is now yours," Ophelia says.

"Mine? Why mine?"

"Because you belong here. I've known it from the start."

Oliver frowns. "Annie can't take that. We'll be happy to stay for as long as you need us, but there's no need—"

Stopping him in mid-thought, Ophelia says, "I know there's no need. I'm doing this because it's what I want to."

"Why?" Annie asks. "Why all of a sudden do you want—"

"It's not all of a sudden," Ophelia says. She explains she has decided to take an apartment at Baylor Towers where she can be with friends her own age.

As she listens Annie's eyes fill with tears. "I thought we were friends."

Ophelia pulls Annie into her arms. "We're more than friends. We're family."

"Well, then why?" Annie says, choking back a sob.

"Because this house was made for lovers. I knew it the first time Edward and I saw it. It's got a magic all its own but it's a magic meant for lovers, not for an old woman who has nothing to cling to but memories."

"But I thought you were happy with your memories—"

"Content," Ophelia says, "but not happy. Happy is when you can laugh out loud and dance as if there is no tomorrow. Happy is when you have your lover lying next to you and the only sound you hear is that of his heartbeat."

Ophelia's eyes fill with water as she remembers.

"Edward and I had our turn at happy," she says. Her voice is soft and tender; it has the sound of a mother talking to her child. "This time belongs to you and Oliver."

"Don't worry about Annie and me," Oliver says. "We've got plenty of time."

Ophelia looks at him and smiles. "I thought that also, but there is never enough time. No matter how many years you have, when the time comes you plead for one more dance, one more kiss, one more time of hearing him say I love you."

AS OPHELIA SPEAKS MAX RISES from her chair and taps the others on the shoulder signaling for them to follow her. As they tiptoe out the door she whispers this is a time when Ophelia, Annie and Oliver need to be alone.

"I've got to call Baylor Towers for the car to pick us up," Sam says.

"That's okay," Max replies. "I'll drive you home."

THE SKY GROWS DARK, BUT the three of them continue to talk. In time they leave the dishes on the table and move to the back porch.

Annie continues to insist she doesn't want the house.

"All I ask is for you to stay here and let us take care of you," she says.

Ophelia can feel Annie's sorrow in her own heart, but she remains firm. "It's too late. The deed has already been transferred, and I've put a hold on an apartment at Baylor Towers."

When Annie hears this, the tears stream down her cheeks.

"How could you?" she says, her voice harsh and accusing. "How could you leave and not care—"

"Annie!" Oliver says sharply. "Don't do this. Ophelia doesn't deserve—"

Ophelia again signals him to stop. When he does she reaches across and takes Annie's hand in hers.

"Don't ever think I don't care," she says. "I do. I care more for you than I've cared for anyone since I lost my dear sweet Edward. You've made me remember the joy of living."

Annie blinks back the tears. "Then why?"

"Because you've got a life to live, and so do I," Ophelia says. "It's wrong to let love be a reason for not living life to the fullest—"

"But—"

"There are no buts. It's already been decided. I'm going to live at Baylor Towers. Now if you care for me half as much as I do you, you'll help me move in and get settled."

When Annie looks up, she sees Oliver waiting for her answer just as Ophelia is. At that moment she remembers what he said when, instead of continuing on their honeymoon, he willingly turned the car around and headed back to Virginia.

I'm hoping that one day you will love me the way you do Ophelia.

The hope in his eyes wraps itself around her heart. She smiles at him, then gives Ophelia's hand an affectionate squeeze.

"Of course I'll help you," she says. The anger is gone from her words.

MAX

Whoa, I never saw that coming. I feel bad enough that it's the end of my project, but I feel even worse for Annie. I know how excited she was about this evening. She fussed over every detail of that dinner because she wanted it to be perfect. She wasn't looking for something in return; she just really loves Ophelia.

This is probably hard for her to understand right now, but after I drove Lillian and her friends back to Baylor Towers I could see why Ophelia wants to live there. Those folks might be a bit older, but they sure know how to have fun. Sam is a hoot. The whole way home he was telling dumb jokes. At first I thought they were kind of cornball, you know, the stuff nobody laughs at. But by the time we got to the building, I was in stitches.

Ophelia loves Annie; she showed it by giving her the house. Somebody who doesn't care a bean about you doesn't up and give you a house. Right now Annie's feelings are hurt so she can't see it. Once she gets over her hurt, she'll realize what a nice thing Ophelia did.

It's like having an ice cream cone with two scoops. If the top ball falls off, you feel so bad about it you forget you've still got the cone with another scoop of ice cream inside.

My losing this project was the top ball falling, but having Annie as a friend means I've still got the cone and the second scoop.

Nothing is all good or all bad; that's how you've got to look at life. If you see it from one side or the other, you're just going to make yourself crazy.

BAYLOR TOWERS

The weekend passes with no further mention of the move. But on Monday morning when the three of them sit down to breakfast, Ophelia says she plans to see the apartment today. She looks across at Annie and asks, "Will you go with me, or should I call for a car?"

Oliver peers over the edge of his cup and waits for Annie's answer.

"I'll go," she says. She doesn't say she'll be happy to go, just that she'll go.

This answer is enough to please Oliver. He smiles then reaches beneath the table and gives her knee a squeeze.

He scoops up the last few bites of his omelet and stands. "I've got a full docket, so I won't be back until after six." He kisses Annie on the mouth, gives Ophelia a peck on the cheek and is gone.

Oliver has been a buffer, a wall holding back Annie's sorrow and softening the pain of Ophelia's words. Now it is just the two of them. For a moment there is an uncomfortable silence. It is a moment that could easily segue into either acceptance or anger.

Annie is first to speak. "Since we're already going to be at

Baylor Towers, maybe you could call your friend Lillian and ask if she'd like to have lunch with us."

A broad smile crosses Ophelia's face. "That's a wonderful idea. It'll be my treat."

Annie gives a guilty grin. "Actually it's Oliver's treat. He was the one who suggested it."

Although Ophelia says only that she must remember to thank him, inside her chest she can feel her heart swelling to twice its size.

THE BUILDING IS EXACTLY AS OPHELIA imagined. Tall and stately with a burgundy awning covering the walkway. A uniformed doorman greets them when they step inside. Ophelia gives her name and he buzzes for the building manager, Peter Peters.

Peters is there within minutes and welcomes them with a handshake. "Call me Pete," he says. "Everyone does."

They cross the lobby and take the elevator to the second floor. Pete unlocks the door and they step inside. The apartment is just as it appeared in the pictures: a tiny kitchen where the refrigerator and stove are an arm's length from one another. A breakfast nook large enough for a small table and perhaps four chairs, far too small for the mahogany dining room set. That Ophelia will leave behind.

In the center of the apartment is a fairly spacious living room. It is large enough to accommodate most of the parlor furniture, including the bookcase. At the end of the room a sliding glass door opens onto a small terrace overlooking the flower gardens.

Ophelia catches the fragrance of the garden and smiles.

"It's lovely," she says with satisfaction. Already she can picture where she will set the chintz sofa and the comfy leather chair.

The single bedroom is small, much smaller than the loft. She will bring the small dresser and the mattress she and Edward slept on. It is old and should be replaced, but on certain nights she can still catch the smell of his cologne so she will hold on to it. The bed itself is a built-in platform, nailed to the floor, so it will remain behind.

One by one Ophelia imagines each of her things in its new spot in this apartment. A lamp in the corner. Her special potpourri on a small table by the door. A tiny nightstand alongside the bed.

After she has gone through the apartment, Ophelia signs the lease and lists Annie as her next of kin. In the spot where the questionnaire asks relationship she writes "Very close," which oddly enough is the best possible explanation.

Pete hands Ophelia a folder filled with maps and lists. "This will familiarize you with the building layout and the services we offer." He pulls a yellow highlighter from his pocket and circles a telephone number. "This is the number you call for our car service. They'll take you wherever you want to go."

"That's really great," Annie says and gives Ophelia a sly smile. "At least I won't have to worry about you venturing out alone again."

After Pete hands Ophelia the key to her new apartment, he accompanies them back to the lobby. The doorman buzzes Lillian and says her guests are here.

When Lillian arrives in the lobby she is grinning like the Cheshire cat.

"If you have time we'd like to take you to lunch," Annie says.

"I know," Lillian replies. "Oliver already called."

She leads them down a wide hallway. "We have a tradition here at Baylor Towers. When a newcomer arrives we like to welcome them properly." They step through a door onto an open terrace.

Under the awning is a buffet table loaded with bowls of salad and plates of food. When Lillian gives a wave, the group echoes in unison, "Welcome to Baylor!"

Ophelia scans the faces in the crowd and sees Sam and Pauline along with the other friends she's met during the weeks at Kipling. A smile curls the corners of her mouth and she murmurs, "Oh my, what a wonderful surprise."

Annie wants to find fault with Baylor Towers. She wants to dislike the people who are taking Ophelia from her, but it is impossible. They are warm-hearted and friendly. As Ophelia moves about the room chatting with one person and then another she somehow looks younger, like the years have fallen away.

Sam tells a joke and Ophelia laughs. The sound is almost musical. It is a sound not burdened with the weight of sadness, and for that Annie is thankful.

The party continues for most of the afternoon, and when they finally leave Annie can understand why Ophelia wants to live here.

Baylor Towers is making Ophelia a part of it, just as Annie has become a part of Memory House.

ONE WEEK LATER A MOVING van pulls into the driveway of Memory House. A broad-chested man with hands the size of ham hocks knocks at the door and asks if this is the Browne residence.

Ophelia nods. She hands him the list she has prepared and points to the boxes sitting in the living room. They are packed and ready to go. She is leaving her collection of treasures behind. The bicycle, the ball, the raggedy doll, the Lannigan Bible, all of the things containing the memories of other people will remain here at Memory House. It is where they belong.

Ophelia knows Annie will care for them, watch over them and hold them dear, just as she has done for all these many years.

THE FIRST NIGHT

Annie and Ophelia are already at the apartment when the moving van arrives. As the men carry in the odd bits of furniture, the apartment begins to look like a miniaturized version of Memory House. Ophelia slides the glass door open, and the fragrance of flowers floats in. Only the splashing of ducks in the pond is missing. Although it is a sound she has grown used to, it is something she can easily do without.

Once the movers are gone, the two women set to work unpacking the boxes. It is not a difficult job because there are only twelve cartons and a tall wardrobe box. The apartment is small with only one large closet in the bedroom, a tiny linen closet in the bath and a single wall of cupboards in the kitchen. With this in mind, Ophelia has brought only the things she needs: a handful of silverware, six dishes, two sets of sheets and a small stack of towels. The rest she has left behind at Memory House.

By five o'clock the towels are hung, the bed is made and all of the boxes have been emptied. Ophelia plops down on the sofa.

"Whew," she says. "I'm bushed."

"Relax for a while," Annie says. "I'll make a pot of tea then run out and pick up a few groceries."

A tin of dandelion tea was one of the things Ophelia deemed necessary. The various teas, along with her jars of herbs and spices, fill the bottom shelf of the corner cupboard.

"That sounds lovely." Ophelia pushes against the back of her leather chair, and the footrest comes up. She leans into the soft leather and closes her eyes. It is just for a minute, she tells herself, but when Annie returns with the tea she is sound asleep.

Annie quietly slips out and heads to the grocery store. It is less than a block away so she walks.

The store called Baylor Grocery is like a miniature supermarket. They have almost anything a person could ask for, but it is all pared down to single-serving proportions. Wheelbarrow-sized bins of fresh vegetables are nowhere to be seen; instead there are small baskets of fruits and vegetables. The tomatoes are bright red and the string beans a vibrant green, as fresh as they would be if pulled from Ophelia's garden.

Annie goes up and down the aisles selecting what she knows Ophelia will need: milk, eggs, bread, cheese, a prepared dinner of baked meatloaf and another of roast turkey.

She leaves the store carrying three shopping bags filled to the brim, more than enough to last for several days. She will be back tomorrow, but until then she wants to make certain Ophelia has what she needs.

Ophelia is still asleep when Annie returns, so she leaves a note saying she has gone home and will be back tomorrow. She explains there are dinners ready to pop in the oven and at the bottom of the note she adds, "I love you and wish you a world of happiness in your new home."

BY THE TIME ANNIE GETS back to Memory House, Oliver is

already home. She catches the smell of roast chicken the moment she opens the door.

"Oliver?" she calls out.

"In the kitchen," he answers.

She follows the sound of his voice and when she spots him with Ophelia's apron wrapped around his waist, she laughs. "What's this?"

"I thought you might not feel like cooking tonight, so I picked up a baguette and a rotisserie chicken. Now I'm making a salad."

Annie crosses over and peers into the bowl. It is filled with chunks of romaine, tomatoes, cucumbers, onions and what looks to be a bit of summer squash. On the cutting board there are partially chopped red and green peppers.

"That's going to be an awfully big salad," she says. "Are we having company?"

"Nope, it's just the two of us." He pulls her into his arms and presses his body to hers. Lowering his mouth to her ear he whispers, "But I've got something special planned."

He leads her outside where he has already spread a blanket on the lawn. Beside it sits a tray with two glasses and a bottle of Pinot Grigio chilling in the ice bucket. He pulls the iPod from his pocket and hits play. The strains of soft instrumentals fill the air; not songs Annie can recognize, just sweet melodies.

"In case you haven't noticed it, we're dining al fresco."

Annie is still wearing the jeans and tee shirt she has been working in all day. "Do I have time for a shower?" she asks.

He nods. "But make it quick. Dinner is in fifteen minutes."

WHILE ANNIE IS SHOWERING, OLIVER arranges a platter with salad on one side and slices of chicken on the other. They will eat from the same dish. He will spear bites of chicken and hold them to her lips, then use his hands to break apart pieces of the baguette for her. He wants this to be more than a meal; he wants this to be the first in a long string of new memories that will make them a part of this house.

Ophelia's words have settled in his heart and he knows they are true; he only hopes he can make Annie believe.

When she returns, Annie is barefoot. Her hair has the scent of fresh strawberries and hangs wet against her shoulders. She wears only a lightweight spaghetti strap dress and her panties.

Oliver gives a look of approval. "Pretty," he says. He kisses her mouth and lowers her to the blanket.

There is no rushing, no sense of urgency. There is only the chilled wine, the sweet sound of music and the moon climbing ever higher into the sky.

ANNIE

I thought the first night without Ophelia here would be heartbreaking, but it wasn't. Having dinner outside on the lawn was like stepping into some sort of fairyland.

I guess Ophelia was right; there is something magical about this house. I've felt it for a long time but always believed the magic was in her, not the house. Oliver, bless his heart, was wise enough to see the truth.

To me the loft seemed like Ophelia and Edward's special place, sort of a hallowed ground that strangers shouldn't trample on. But this morning after Oliver left for work I went up there and looked around. The bookshelves are empty and the mattress is gone, so now it just feels like a big empty room. When Ophelia moved out, all her memories went with her.

I guess that's how it's supposed to be. Treasured memories are meant to stay with the person they belong to. Only the scattered memories with trouble stuck to them stay behind, waiting for someone like me to someday stumble on them.

After last night I've decided to let myself be happy here. I know it's what Ophelia wants, and now I can see it's what Oliver wants also.

I'm going to buy a mattress and turn the loft into our bedroom.

Oliver may not be able to name the stars, but that certainly doesn't lessen the pleasure of lying there and looking up at them.

Living in this house makes people do things they never thought they'd do, and Ophelia claims that's a good thing.

I certainly hope she's right.

A TIME OF CHANGES

Before a month has passed, the changes begin. Ophelia settles into Baylor Towers as if she'd been born there. She joins the Garden Club and volunteers to make three floral arrangements for the Fall Festival Luncheon. She also buys a 21-inch television and the stand that goes with it.

Every afternoon at three o'clock she raises the footrest of the leather chair and clicks on channel six. "Don't call me when the Ellen Show is on," she tells Annie.

DURING THE FIRST FEW WEEKS Annie called or came to visit every day, but now she also is busy. With Max's help she is trying to figure out what to do with the loft.

At first she thought it was simply a question of ordering a new mattress, but once the mattress is delivered she realizes this is not enough. Something is wrong, but what it is she cannot say.

When Oliver suggests they sleep in the loft, she claims it is too soon. And on three different occasions when Ophelia asks if they have moved into the loft, Annie shakes her head no.

"What are you waiting for?" Ophelia asks.

Annie explains that she feels like an intruder.

"It's almost like I don't belong there," she says. "Like I'm trying to fit into someone else's shoes."

Ophelia laughs. "That's because you haven't made the room your own. Edward built that room for us; now you've got to rebuild it for you and Oliver."

"Rebuild it?"

"Yes. Change everything. Pare it down to the bare walls and start over."

"I can't. The bed is built in and—"

"That's not a bed," Ophelia says, chuckling. "It's just a platform Edward topped with a mattress. A few boards nailed to the floor, that's all."

In Annie's mind the platform had been a sacred altar, something to be revered and left untouched.

"You mean you wouldn't mind if I changed it?" she asks.

"Of course not."

"But you said you wanted Memory House to always remain the same."

"No, I said I want it to stay the same in my memory, and it will. Anything you do now won't change the picture in my mind."

Ophelia smiles and the flood of memories begins. "It's long past time for that platform to go," she says. "When we began sleeping in the loft every night, Edward promised he would replace it with a real bed." She gives a nostalgic sigh. "He just never got the chance."

This thought settles in Annie's mind and gives her renewed inspiration.

On a Tuesday morning when there is a mist of rain in the air and fog surrounds the house like a low lying cloud, Annie brews a tea said to inspire creative thought. It is a bitter mix of yarrow and mugwort, but she adds clover honey to sweeten the taste.

When the drink is ready, she pours it into a large mug and carries it to the loft.

She tugs the new mattress from its base, leans it against the wall, then sits cross-legged on the wooden platform. She is determined to reimagine the room as one for her and Oliver.

Little by little the picture comes. The walls change from a faded beige to a blue the color of a late afternoon sky. The pale oak floor takes on the sheen of ripened black cherries. Sheer curtains hang at the side window and puddle on the floor. Hours pass before Annie can imagine the platform bed gone, but once she does a beautiful mahogany Queen Anne bed easily enough replaces it. *Perfect,* she thinks and fixes the picture in her mind.

That afternoon she calls Max.

"I'm going to need your help," she says. "Bring paint brushes and a crowbar."

The project takes a full three weeks to complete. They start by prying the boards of the platform bed from the floor. Already the room seems larger. Once the platform is gone, Annie fills the nail holes with wood putty and rents a sander.

Throughout the week Max is there to help, and on weekends Oliver steps in. It takes three days of sanding before the floor is ready for stain. By then Annie has repainted the walls, and Max has turned the unfinished bookcase into the white of a cloud.

Once the floor is stained and varnished, it needs another three days to dry. That evening Annie and Oliver talk about furniture.

"I'm picturing a Queen Anne bed," she says. "Something like this." She flips open a folder and produces an ad clipped from *Architectural Digest.*

Oliver raises an eyebrow and wrinkles his forehead. "Hmmm."

"Hmmm what?" Annie says.

"Well, I was thinking we'd use some of my furniture from the townhouse."

A look of hesitation settles on her face. "I don't think it's exactly..."

"You don't have to decide right now," he says. "Drive over tomorrow by yourself, and take your time looking around. Once you get the feel of the place, you can figure out whether that furniture will work here or not."

She nods. "Fair enough."

Oliver has seen the folder, and other than the Queen Anne bed the pictures inside are almost exactly the same as the furniture Ophelia took with her. He hopes Annie's vision of what the rooms should look like will be swayed by memories of their time spent at the townhouse.

"Are you sure you don't want to come with me?" she asks.

"I've got a full docket for the next two weeks," he says, "but I trust your judgment."

THE NEXT MORNING ANNIE TACKS a note on the apothecary door saying she'll be back by four, then climbs into her car and heads for Wyattsville.

Up until now she has been so preoccupied with the loft she has given little thought to the empty living room, the missing table in the hall or the breakfast nook with nothing but a single chair.

When she parks her car in the townhouse driveway and unlocks the front door, it is like opening a treasure chest of memories.

The warmth of Oliver's smile when he introduced his dad, her long sought bicycle boy, is here in this room. She can still picture Ethan Allen sitting in the wing back chair and Ophelia across from him. The Christmas tree with its tiny white lights winking and blinking like the merriest of elves. The stereo spilling sounds of joy.

She walks to the bookshelves, two tall cherry wood cabinets standing side by side, a graceful duo for sure. She runs her hand along the spine of several books, tales of heroic men, books filled with knowledge, so many stories. By the time her fingers touch *The Wisdom of Judicial Judgment in the Practice of Law*, Annie knows she wants to bring this entire room to Memory House. How could she not? Every splinter of wood is filled with memories, some that she and Oliver have already made and some that are waiting to be discovered.

It is the same in the bedroom. How, she wonders, could she have ever imagined a Queen Anne bed in the loft? This bed, the one they slept in on their wedding night, is obviously perfect. And the dresser, such a wonderful match. It would be criminal not to take that and the nightstands as well.

After she has gone through the entire townhouse, Annie has eliminated only a brown leather chair that is too big to move anyway and a vacuum cleaner with a broken hose.

THAT EVENING AS ANNIE AND Oliver sit across from one another at the dinner table she gives a nostalgic sigh.

"I can't imagine why we ever considered selling all those beautiful things at the townhouse," she says.

"Neither can I," Oliver says with a twinkle in his eye. "Neither can I."

A Perfect Life

On Thursday of the following week, a moving van pulls into the driveway of Memory House and unloads the furniture from Oliver's townhouse. Annie points to the precise spot where every item is to be placed, and by early afternoon the house is exactly as she imagined it.

Well, perhaps not exactly. There are still odds and ends to be done: unpack the boxes, set books on the shelves, hang the curtains and find a spot where the painting of the Wyattsville courthouse can be hung.

The side room that was once Ophelia's sewing den is now Oliver's study.

Although it is smaller than the study at the townhouse, everything fits. Annie unpacks the desk accessories, then sets to polishing the furniture. She is pondering the arrangement of things when the cowbell clangs and Max comes charging in.

"I knocked, but I guess you didn't hear." She offers a bottle of Merlot. "I figured tonight's the night, so this is to go with dinner."

Annie takes the bottle. "Thanks, but tonight's not the night. Tomorrow is. I want everything to be perfect, and there's still a lot to do." She rattles off a list of still-to-be done chores.

"Can Oliver help with some of that stuff?"

Annie shakes her head. "He'd be glad to, but with Judge Cooper on vacation he doesn't even have time for lunch."

Max peels off her jacket and tosses it on the chair. "I'm not busy. I'll lend a hand."

ONCE EVEN THE TINIEST FLECK of dust is gone from the office, they move to the other rooms. Cleaning. Polishing. Shining every surface until it gleams. It is almost six when they finish the downstairs.

Max drops onto the sofa and casts an eye around the room.

"The place looks terrific," she says. "So different from the way it was."

It is as Ophelia said. Annie and Oliver are no longer intruders; Memory House is now their home. Pieces of their life are visible in the farthest corner of every room. The sweetness of Ophelia's memory is still here, but now it is simply a memory.

"Wait until you see the loft," Annie says.

Max follows Annie up the stairs. When she peers into the room she sees the stacks of boxes to be unpacked, curtains waiting to be hung and the ticking of a queen-size mattress that is yet to be covered, but already she can envision the room as it will be.

"Amazing," she exclaims.

Annie gives a dreamy-eyed grin. "This is going to be the best weekend of my life," she says. "Tomorrow I'm going to finish this room and make a lamb stew, Oliver's favorite. Then we'll sleep here under the stars."

"Sounds like a perfect night," Max replies.

"More like a perfect life," Annie corrects her. "Saturday is the dinner party. You're coming aren't you?"

Max nods. "You bet I am."

"Good. That makes eight. Giselle and Bill, the Jacksons, Andrew, you—"

"Wait a minute," Max says. "Andrew who?"

"Andrew Steen. Andy was Oliver's partner in the law firm. He's really sweet and good-looking. Actually he—"

"This isn't a blind date, is it?" Max asks suspiciously.

"Of course not," Annie says. "But I wouldn't be too disappointed if the two of you happened to hit it off."

Max scrunches her nose into a look of disdain. "It sounds like a fix-up! You know I've sworn off love. It's fine for you, but it doesn't work for me."

"I know," Annie replies. The sly grin on her face is a sharp contrast to her words.

ON FRIDAY WHEN THE LAST courtroom session ends, Oliver returns to his office. His face is lined and weary. It has been a long week with too many difficult decisions. Next week promises to be no better. An ever-growing stack of files sits on the corner of his desk calling for attention. *Not tonight,* he thinks. He scans the folders, selects several of the most critical cases and tucks them into his briefcase.

Over the weekend he'll find time to review them, but tonight he's promised Annie he'll come home early.

WHEN OLIVER OPENS THE DOOR, the smell of a bubbling lamb stew greets him. The fragrance comes partly from the stew itself and partly from the hallway potpourri. Annie has promised lamb stew, and he is already thinking of it.

"I'm home," he calls out.

Annie comes from the kitchen carrying two glasses of red wine. Oliver drops the bulging briefcase alongside the chest of drawers in the hall and takes a glass from her hand.

"Well, now," he says with a chuckle, "this is just what I need."

Annie stretches up and kisses his mouth. "Welcome to what is going to be the best weekend of our lives."

There is the clink of glass against glass as they toast the thought.

AS THEY SHARE A SECOND glass of wine, Oliver's concerns of the courtroom fade away. He sets aside the images of haggard parents with sorrowful faces, children bristling with anger and advocates with worried brows.

"Ophelia was right," he tells Annie. "There is a certain magic to this house." He chuckles again. "You thought the magic was in her…"

Annie stands at the stove stirring the pot. He takes the spoon from her hand, sets it aside and pulls her body into his. He lowers his face to hers, close enough for her to feel the heat of his breath on her cheek.

"But I think the magic is in you," he whispers, then covers her mouth with his in a kiss that envelopes Annie completely.

She can think of nothing sweeter than having such a kiss last through all of eternity.

When he pulls back she says, "If we don't eat dinner now, we may not get to it tonight…"

Oliver gives a hearty laugh. "Asking a man to choose between you and the lamb stew is totally unfair!"

"Not choose." Her lashes flutter as she curls her mouth into a seductive smile. "Just prioritize."

THE SKY IS DARK AND the air has grown chilly when they sit down to dinner on the back porch. Candles light the table and the stew is bubbling hot, but the silverware is icy cold to the touch.

"I'm afraid we won't be able to have too many more dinners out here," Annie says. As the words leave her mouth an ominous shiver slides up her spine, and she winces.

Oliver notices. "Silly girl. This is never going to end. When we're ninety and there's a crust of snow covering the ground, we'll pull on parkas and toddle out here with our steamy mugs of hot chocolate."

He laughs and she laughs with him.

LATER THAT NIGHT AS THEY lie in bed looking up at the stars, Annie knows this place now belongs to them.

"I wonder if we've made a baby tonight," she murmurs.

"If not," Oliver whispers, "we can try again tomorrow night and the night after and the night after that…"

Given such a thought, Annie snuggles deeper into his arms. "If it's a girl, let's call her Starr."

"And if it's a boy we'll call him Moon. Moon Doyle, now that's a good football player's name."

Annie pokes her elbow into his ribs and giggles.

As they lie there in the bed it is as if all their tomorrows are stretched out before them. It is a new galaxy to travel, a lifetime to get where they are going. By the time they drift off to sleep, the rose color of dawn is already seeping into the sky.

THE DINNER PARTY

On Saturday morning Annie wakes to the splatter of raindrops against the skylight. She snuggles back under the comforter, then remembers the dinner party they have planned.

"Ugh, got to get moving," she encourages herself sleepily.

She sits up and tries to rub the sleep from her eyes, but before she can push herself any further Oliver throws his arm across her chest and pulls her back down.

"Not yet," he whispers and kisses her shoulder.

The aura of sleep is still wrapped around him, and it sucks her in.

"I have to get things ready for the party." Her words have no protest; they are simply a thought that came to mind.

"Stay with me," Oliver says. "I'll help do whatever it is later on."

Annie rolls onto her side facing him. For a few moments she lets herself soak up the beauty of this man who is the whole of her world; then she lazily closes her eyes and lowers her head into the valley of his neck.

IT IS CLOSE TO NOON when they finally climb from the bed. Annie pulls on a pair of jeans and a tee shirt. Oliver takes a quick shower; she doesn't. The truth is she likes the smell of him that lingers on her skin.

Even though there is a chill in the air and rain still drips from the eves, they sit on the back porch to have hazelnut coffee and cinnamon biscuits.

Annie looks across at Oliver, his hair still wet from the shower, his smile soft and easy.

"Tell me again," she says. "Tell me how when we're ninety we'll still be as we are today."

He laughs. "We won't be exactly as we are today. My hair will be silver, and you'll have laugh lines in the corners of your eyes but, ah, what wonderful memories we'll have."

Annie smiles and leans into his words.

"We'll cover ourselves with a woolen lap robe and bask in the glow of all that we've gone through together." He gives a raucous laugh. "Like remembering the time when we invited all those people for dinner and never got ready."

Annie jumps up. "Oh, my gosh, we'd better get moving."

WHEN THE GUESTS ARRIVE AT seven, Annie is showered and dressed. In the oven are eight tiny Cornish hens stuffed with rice. The table is set with the Rosenthal china handed down from Edward's mother to Ophelia and from Ophelia to Annie.

Outside of Ophelia's welcome home dinner party, which turned out to be a disaster, this is the first dinner party Annie has ever prepared. She has fussed over every tiny detail. Made place cards for each guest, set out a tray of wines and liquors, and followed line-by-line instructions in the Betty Crocker cookbook. Although she is perfectly at home mixing herbs and potions in the apothecary, she is a nervous wreck preparing a dinner such as this.

MAX IS THE FIRST TO arrive. "Am I too early?"

Annie shakes her head. "Not at all. I could use an extra hand to help serve these hors d'oeuvres."

Gisele and Bill arrive at the same time as the Jacksons, and by the time Oliver opens the door they've introduced themselves to one another. Harry and Francine Jackson own the townhouse next door to Oliver's.

Andrew is the last to arrive. He comes with a bouquet of flowers and a bottle of wine. When he is introduced to Max she is carrying a tray of hors d'oeuvres and his hands are both full, so they each give a cordial nod and keep moving.

A short while later Max corners Annie in the kitchen about Andrew.

"The poor guy doesn't know what to say," she says. "He thinks this is a fix up. Did you tell him I'm not the least bit interested in anything that's even remotely romantic?"

"Of course I did," Annie says. "He's just a kind of shy person."

"A lawyer who's shy?" Max laughs. "Now *that's* an oxymoron."

"I heard that," Andrew says, appearing suddenly. He hands Annie the flowers. "I thought you might want to put these in a vase."

"I'm sorry," Max stutters. "I wasn't trying to—"

"No problem," Andrew says with a grin. "But just for the record, I'm not the least bit interested in anything remotely romantic either."

Once he leaves the room Max looks around to make certain no one is behind her this time, then lets go of loud whoosh of air.

"That was uncomfortable to say the least."

Annie smiles. "I don't think Andrew's angry. It sounded like he kind of thought it was funny."

Even as she says this, Annie thinks perhaps she should

rearrange the place cards indicating where each person should sit.

When they finally sit down to dinner, Andrew is at the far end of the table on the opposite side from Max.

OTHER THAN THAT TINY LITTLE moment of awkwardness, the evening goes smoothly. Everyone raves about the dinner, and Oliver brags of Annie's many talents.

"It's a lucky man who can find beauty and brains in one package," he quips. Before the evening ends Annie knows the dinner party has been a success. Everyone exchanges phone numbers, and they leave claiming they must do this again soon.

"Very soon," Annie and Oliver echo as they wave goodbye to the last of the guests.

Although the hour is late and she is up to her elbows in a pan of soapy water with the last of the dishes, Annie has never been happier. Gone are the lonely nights, the pretense of being someone other than herself, the heartaches. Now there is only the promise of a future more wonderful than anything she could have ever imagined.

ANNIE

You're not going to believe this, but a little over a year ago I was a total mess. I thought I was in love with Michael, a man who thought way more of himself than he did of me. A man like that tells you you're worthless and lucky to stand in his shadow; then before long he has you believing it's true.

The day Michael walked out on me was the luckiest day of my life. I didn't think so at the time, but looking back I know for sure it was.

I would have never come to Memory House if not for that.

Once I got to know Ophelia and started to learn about the magic of memories, I couldn't wait to get here each weekend and see what new adventure was in store for me. I thought surely those were the best days of my life.

Then I met Oliver.

Now I know for certain these are the best days of my life.

I never dreamed love could be so wonderful. If a fairy godmother walked up to me right this minute and said she'd grant any wish I wanted, I couldn't think of a single thing to wish for. I've got everything I'll ever need to be happy.

Nothing, and I truly do mean nothing, could ever spoil this

happiness Oliver and I have. When you have a love like this, you feel like you're the richest woman in the world.

When he talks about how we are going to grow old together, I feel like I'm living in a fairy tale. Only this time I get to be the princess.

THE WEIGHT OF HAPPINESS

Once a stone has been added to the scale of life, it can never be removed. This is the law laid down before the dawn of time. Centuries upon centuries have passed, and still the law stands. There has never been an exception, and no one has ever dared to challenge what is known only as the law.

The Keeper of the Scale knew this when he added the rose-colored stone to the happiness side of Annie's scale. He looked into the future and saw what was to come, but at the time he believed the loneliness and sorrow of her early years were weighty enough to hold the scale in balance. Now he has come to regret his actions.

No one, not even the Keeper of the Scale, could foretell a happiness so great it would topple the scale itself.

The Keeper eyed Annie's scale with a steely grey eye and rubbed his hand across his chin. He lifted a cluster of small river stones into his hand and dropped the first one onto the side of sorrow. The scale remained as it was.

He dropped a second stone. Then a third, a fourth and a fifth. Still Annie's happiness remained unshakable. He finally lifted the jagged black rock into his hand, and with a sigh so mournful it caused the earth to tremble he dropped the stone onto the side of sorrow.

THE PREMONITION

On Monday morning when Oliver kisses Annie goodbye, he warns he might be late getting home.

"I need to spend some time going over Cooper's case files," he says.

"If it gets too late, be sure to call me," Annie replies.

Her brows are pinched and the right side of her mouth tucked tight, because for some strange and totally unexplainable reason she has developed a worrisome tick in her head.

Oliver chucks her under the chin. "Don't worry."

Annie stands and watches as he climbs into his car and backs out of the driveway. "Right," she mumbles. "What is there to worry about?"

In her mind Annie thumbs through a list of things that could possibly go wrong this day, and still she finds nothing.

She turns back inside the house and walks from room to room as though there is something she has missed, but still there is nothing. No leftover boxes left to unpack, no piece of furniture stuck in the wrong place, no drawer left hanging open. But still the feeling of uneasiness is stuck in her chest. Some troublesome thing tugs at her heart.

Today there is work to do in the apothecary. She has three drying racks filled with herbs, leaves, roots and vines. They all need to be mulled, crushed into granules and mixed together. She is in the middle of carving a piece of ginger root into chunks when the feeling comes again.

It's not a memory. It's a premonition.

Something is not as it should be.

Annie leaves the apothecary and walks through the house a second time; that's when she sees Oliver's briefcase standing alongside the chest of drawers in the front hall.

"That's it!" she exclaims.

She dials his cell phone number. It rings five times; then the message clicks on. "I am unavailable…"

Annie pushes "End" and doesn't bother leaving a message. Instead she grabs a sweater from the closet, picks up the briefcase and climbs into her car. When she backs out of the driveway, she is smiling. She can already picture the delight on Oliver's face when she walks in and hands him the forgotten briefcase.

It is after ten by the time she arrives at the courthouse. Oliver's court is already in session.

"If this is an emergency, I can pass Judge Doyle a note and let him know you're here," the clerk says.

Disappointment is written across Annie's face, but she says it is not an emergency. She hands the clerk the briefcase.

"He went off without this," she says. "Could you see that he gets it?"

"Absolutely." The clerk nods.

Annie thanks him and walks away. Not seeing Oliver is a disappointment but nothing to be alarmed about. She is on her way back to the elevator when she turns and walks toward room 203. Just beneath the room number, his nameplate has been slid into place: Judge Oliver Doyle. On the bench across the hall there is a young mother with two children. They all sit in silence, the girl with her head in the woman's lap, the boy sucking his thumb as he clings to his mother.

For a moment Annie considers slipping into the courtroom and watching, but it seems an invasion. Oliver has said custody battle judgments are often heart wrenching and difficult to sort through; she is certain seeing her there would make it more so.

WHEN ANNIE LEAVES THE COURTHOUSE she checks her watch. It is only ten-thirty. Although she has a fair bit of work to do at the apothecary, the day in front of her now seems longer, emptier and more stretched out.

Since she is already in Wyattsville, she telephones Max.

"Have you got time to go for coffee?" she asks. "I've got something I'd like to talk about."

"Sorry," Max says. "My client wants these drawings by four o'clock. If it's something important, I can stop by the house later."

"Nothing important," Annie says. "We can catch up tomorrow."

ON THE WAY HOME ANNIE takes the long route, the one that circles around Wyattsville and past Baylor Towers. Since she is already there she stops in to see Ophelia.

The doorman buzzes Ophelia's apartment, but there is no answer.

"I think she's in the card room," he says. "You can go on back if you'd like."

Annie shakes her head. "It's nothing important. I'll catch her next time."

The truth is that it is nothing important. It's simply that she can't shake this premonition hanging over her head. She knows if kept secret inside your heart, a worry can feed on itself and grow to unimaginable proportions. Once shared, it is usually exposed for the meaningless thing it is.

The only problem is right now she can't find anyone with whom to share it.

ANNIE SPENDS THE AFTERNOON IN the apothecary. Three customers come in, chat for a while then leave. Still the day stretches on.

Each minute seems like an hour, and the hours weigh upon her as if they are weeks or even months. Now that the house is finished and the garden readied for winter, there is little to do.

She mulls and mixes the last of the dried leaves, rearranges the tiny jars on the shelves and mixes a new potpourri. This one has the musky smell of Oliver's aftershave.

When she can find nothing more to do, Annie snaps off the light in the apothecary and goes back to the kitchen. It is already seven, a time when she'd ordinarily have dinner on the stove, but she waits. Oliver has said he will call when he is on his way home. It is a forty-minute drive, so she'll have time enough for cooking dinner.

Annie fixes herself a cup of dandelion tea then takes *To Kill a Mockingbird* from the shelf and starts to read. She has read the book countless times, yet it is still a pleasure. She adores Scout and hopes she and Oliver will one day have a daughter who is just like her—bright, fearless and inquisitive.

IT IS ALMOST EIGHT WHEN Oliver leaves the courthouse. He has much on his mind, but Ella Mae Grimley is at the forefront of those thoughts. He cannot dismiss the thought of how the children clung to her. The boy, five years old and still sucking his thumb. The girl, only four and so shy she speaks in barely a whisper. Ella Mae pleading to keep her children. Margaret Grimly, an angry mother-in-law, arguing Ella Mae is unfit.

"No income," Margaret's lawyer argued. "No job, no permanent residence."

All of this is true, but still the kids cling to Ella Mae and cry not to be taken away.

Ella Mae's only proponent is a public defender who until this morning never laid eyes on her. He argues that Margaret's son dying of a drug overdose does not make Ella Mae an unfit mother.

Oliver knows there are probably a thousand other things the lawyer could have said in the girl's defense, but the truth is he hasn't taken the time to find them.

The knife-edged facts point one way, but beyond those facts is the truth. That truth is what Oliver struggles to find.

He is halfway home when he remembers to call Annie.

DANNY LARSON IS A MAN who likes to drink, but he doesn't consider himself a drunk. All right, tonight he's had too many whiskeys, but it's understandable. Given his circumstances, any man would do the same. It's the only thing you can do when you come home in the middle of the afternoon and find your wife with another man.

"I'M SORRY," ANITA HAD SAID. "I didn't want you to find out this way."

Had she pleaded for his forgiveness, Danny would have given it. Begrudgingly perhaps, but still, he would have given it to save their marriage.

The thing was she didn't even ask for forgiveness. She didn't try to say it was just a fling, something that meant nothing to her. She shamelessly turned away and said it was inevitable he'd find out sooner or later.

There was nothing else Danny could do. He scraped up the tiny bit of pride he had left and stormed out the door.

"Be gone when I get back!" he'd yelled.

He climbed back into his truck and roared off. With tears blurring his vision and a crack splitting his heart wide open, he'd gone directly to McGivney's and drank whiskey after whiskey. It didn't change anything, but it dulled the pain of knowing.

AFTER HE'S LOST COUNT OF the number of whiskeys he's downed, he lays his head on the bar and sobs like a baby. That's when McGivney cuts him off.

"You've had enough," McGivney says. "Go home. Get some rest. Tomorrow you'll see things in a different light."

"Home?" Danny slobbers. "I ain't ever going home!"

"Well, you're not staying here," McGivney replies. He comes around the bar, pulls Danny off the stool and walks him to the door.

"Want me to call you a cab?" McGivney asks.

"Hell no," Danny says and staggers down the street.

The truck is parked around the corner, half a block down, but before Danny gets to it he stops at the Liquor Depot and buys a quart bottle of Jack Daniels. He opens the bottle as soon as he steps outside the store.

AS DANNY LARSON PULLS AWAY from the curb, he pictures Anita's head under his right foot and stomps down hard on the gas pedal. He thumps over the curb at the corner of Butler Street, sideswipes a Honda, then turns down Wanamaker. As he roars through the intersection at Carlson, he has the bottle tipped to his mouth and doesn't see the light change from yellow to red. The likelihood is even if he had seen it, he wouldn't have given a damn.

OLIVER PULLS THE CELL PHONE from his pocket. For a second, perhaps less than a second, his eyes are lowered. He pushes the speed dial button, and at that moment he feels the impact.

The phone flies from his hand as the side of his car caves in.

There is the rending screech of metal against metal. A scream shatters the air.

Oliver feels the airbag slam into his face, the steering wheel against his chest. His car spins and slides across the road. When it slams into the curb, it rolls over and comes to rest on the grassy lot at the far corner of Wanamaker and Carlson. Pieces of metal ripped from his car are scattered across the intersection.

"OH SHIT," DANNY MOANS AND staggers down from the cab of his truck. His thought is to get the hell out of here as quick as possible. Before he reaches the sidewalk, he collapses into a heap.

ANNIE

I can't imagine why I do this, let some silly little thought get stuck in my head and then worry myself to pieces over it.

So Oliver forgot his briefcase. It's not the end of the world. If he really needed it, I'm sure he would have called or sent someone to pick it up. Anyway, I took it to his office and that should be the end of that. But somehow I feel it's not.

I've looked all over the house and can't find a single thing that's broken or even out of place. Yet I still have the feeling that I'm missing something. Something I should do, or somebody I'm supposed to call.

Before I came to Memory House I used to feel edgy like this more often than not, but back then I had reason. Now I have no reason. Life is as good as it gets. So why am I worrying?

Maybe it's just a leftover bad habit.

I'm hoping that's all it is.

In Dorchester

Annie is only six pages into her book when she drifts away. Five times she rereads the same sentence. She sets the book aside, rinses her teacup in the sink, then goes to the front window and peers out at the emptiness of the street.

She hopes to see Oliver's car coming down the block, but there is nothing. It is after eight. He's never been this late. She tells herself it's understandable. He has Judge Cooper's caseload added to his own.

Every quarter hour the clock chimes, it is a reminder that another fifteen minutes have passed and still there is no word from Oliver. He has warned her that he is going to be late this evening, so there should be no cause for worry. Right?

Although logic argues there is nothing out of the ordinary, nothing worthy of her concern, she cannot dismiss the feeling of uneasiness that has settled in her chest.

At eight-thirty she calls the Wyattsville courthouse. A recording answers. It tells her the courthouse is open from 8AM until 6PM, but if she knows her party's extension she can enter it now. Annie pushes 318, Oliver's extension number. Another recording answers. This one says there is no one available to take her call, please leave a message.

"It's late," Annie says. "I'm worried about you, call me back."
She sits in the chair alongside the telephone and waits.

KAREN BUSBY LIVES IN THE yellow house next to the empty lot on Carlson Street. It's a fairly quiet neighborhood, and that's how she wants it to remain. After eight hours of waiting on harried customers at the Seven-Eleven, she looks forward to uneventful evenings of watching television.

On this particular night she is settling into the recliner when she hears something that sounds like an explosion outside the house.

"What now?" she groans.

When Karen opens the front door to investigate, she finds a black fender lying at the foot of her stoop.

"What the…"

She looks at the vacant lot, sees Oliver's car turned on its side and gasps.

"Holy crap!"

She ducks back inside and dials 9-1-1.

THE ACCIDENT HAPPENED IN DORCHESTER, a town midway between Wyattsville and Burnsville. No one saw it happen, so there is no one to explain the course of events. There is only Karen's recounting of the sound of it.

"Both the truck and car are smashed," she tells the 9-1-1 operator.

"Is anyone hurt?" the operator asks.

"I would guess so," Karen says. "It's pretty bad out there." She volunteers to go look.

"Hold on."

By the time Karen returns to the phone, the operator already has a call in for both the police and fire rescue.

"One guy is lying in the road, and one's still in his car," Karen reports.

"An ambulance is on the way," the dispatcher replies.

Before Karen hangs up the telephone, she hears the scream of sirens.

A PATROL CAR IS FIRST ON the scene. The senior officer kneels beside Danny and feels for a pulse.

"Check the other car!" he yells to his partner.

Keith Ramsey has been on the job for one week, and the sight of this wreck is making his stomach roll. He pushes back the queasiness he feels and raps on the window of Oliver's car.

"You okay, buddy?" he asks.

Oliver's eyes are open. He blinks but can't move. He can barely breathe. The dashboard is pushed in and the steering wheel pressed against his chest with the weight of an elephant.

"Don't try to move," Keith says. He tries to remember the things he's learned in those weeks of training. *Keep talking to the victim, keep them calm, reassure them help is on the way, get their name, make a personal connection.*

"The EMTs are on their way," Keith says. "Don't worry, we're gonna get you out right away."

Oliver blinks again.

"What's your name?" Keith asks. He works to remember the protocol and doesn't leave time for an answer. "You got somebody you want me to call?"

"Annie..." Oliver says in a hoarse whisper. Her name is still on his lips when his eyes close.

Before the fire department rescue truck comes to a full stop, Keith stands and waves them over. "We need to get this guy out."

Three volunteer firemen jump from the truck and dart over.

"The door's jammed," Keith says and steps back.

Pete, the oldest of the three and a regular on the crew, eyes the car then calls for Bull to bring the Halligan bar and spreader.

"We need to pop this door," he says.

Bull is a dark-haired lad with a neck as thick as a thigh. He comes with the Halligan bar and rams it into the space between the door and the jam. Bull pounds his weight against the bar, and within ten seconds the door is open. Not all the way, but enough for Pete to reach in and feel for Oliver's pulse.

"He's alive," Pete says. The sound of relief is in his words, but it doesn't slow his actions. "Let me get a collar on him, then let's get him out of here."

Although Oliver appears to be unconscious, Pete continues talking to him.

"Don't worry," he says. "You're gonna be okay once we get you outta here. All right now, you're gonna feel me putting a collar on your neck, but it's nothing to be concerned about. This is just to stabilize your head until we can get you to the hospital. Easy now...okay, easy...easy..."

As soon as the collar is on, Pete sees Oliver cannot be moved. His legs are pinned beneath the dashboard. Pete says nothing about this. Instead he shoots off another order and speaks of the positive effort underway.

"Almost there," he says. "Almost there. Another few minutes..."

There is no reply to any of Pete's words. Oliver's eyes are closed.

The first ambulance has already taken Danny Larsen off to the hospital. A second ambulance stands by waiting for Oliver.

Once the collar is in place, Pete tells Bull to use the spreader and get the passenger door open.

"Then get in there and let's roll that dash back," he says.

Within fifteen minutes, the rescue team has both doors off of Oliver's car and they've removed the top with a hydraulic cutter.

Now they can lift Oliver from the wreck. Moving gingerly, they lift him onto a backboard and into the waiting ambulance.

As soon as he is secure, the siren is turned on and the ambulance races toward Mercy Hospital.

PETE LOOKS WORN. CASES LIKE this are tough on him. Not because of the work, but because he remembers the faces. They return at night and haunt his dreams. He prays that this one will live. Tomorrow he will drop by the hospital and ask about him. In some cases it's better not to know, but Pete can't help himself.

Each time he prays this one will make it. Some do. Some don't.

He turns to Keith. "You got the guy's name and address?"

Keith nods. "I'll let the family know."

The sorry truth is that Keith doesn't even know if there is family. He knows nothing but the name the victim spoke. Annie. The car is registered to Oliver Doyle. The address on the registration is in Wyattsville.

At twenty minutes of nine, Keith and his senior officer stand at the door of Oliver's now empty townhouse.

It is only by a quirk of fate that Francine Jackson happens to look out the window and catch sight of the patrol car parked in Oliver's driveway.

Not one to ignore something of such interest, Francine pulls on her bathrobe and trots over. "What's going on?"

"We're looking for someone in the Doyle family," the officer says. "Is there an Annie Doyle?"

"Yes," Francine answers. "But you won't find her here. The Doyles moved."

"Where to?"

Francine is a friend, and she prides herself in being a loyal friend. "What's this all about?" she asks tentatively. If it's anything that means trouble—an overdue parking fine, an expired license, or anything of the sort—Francine is prepared to lie. She'll say to the best of her knowledge they've moved to Kentucky.

"There's been an automobile accident," Keith says solemnly. "We're looking for Mister Doyle's next of kin."

Francine gasps and her hand flies to her mouth. "Oh dear God..."

ONCE THE OFFICERS HAVE THE Burnsville address, they turn the car around and head in that direction.

Francine doesn't know if she should call Annie and tell her, or if something like this is better left to the police. The truth is she knows only that there has been an accident. She knows nothing of what happened.

When she can come to no other decision, Francine calls Max.

"I think you'd better get over there," she says. "I've got a feeling Annie is going to need you."

"I'm on it," Max replies.

Five minutes later Max is driving to Burnsville.

MERCY HOSPITAL

When the clock strikes nine, Annie gives way to the fear bubbling in her stomach. Her first call is to Max, but there is no answer.

Annie doesn't actually expect Max to know where Oliver is. She's simply looking for someone to tell her the fear that's settled in her heart is foolish. Max is sensible and realistic, but Max isn't available.

The next call is to Ophelia.

"Have you heard from Oliver?" she asks.

"Me?" Ophelia says. "Why would I be hearing from Oliver?"

Annie explains the situation.

"Hmm. It could be that he's just busy. Every so often Edward would do that, get busy doing paperwork and not bother to answer the telephone."

She hesitates, remembering how the telephone rang and rang when she called Edward from her mama's house. That time he didn't answer because he was either dead or dying.

"Maybe you should call the police," she tells Annie. "They have access to the courthouse, and they'll go check on him."

The seriousness of Ophelia's tone makes Annie think her fear might be justified. As soon as she hangs up the telephone, she gets out the directory and looks up the number for the Burnsville Police Department. As she is dialing the number, the brass knocker clanks against the front door.

Fear doesn't take logic into consideration. Instead of questioning why Oliver would knock rather than use his key, she says, "Thank God," and runs to the door.

When she flings it open, two officers from the Dorchester police department stand there.

"Annie Doyle?" the older one asks.

A wave of nausea rolls up from her stomach, and she knows this is not good. "Yes?"

"There's been an automobile accident," he says. "Your husband..."

He continues talking. His lips move, but Annie hears only snippets. "Drunk." "Injured. "Mercy Hospital."

None of it makes any sense to Annie. Oliver is a good driver, a sensible driver. He's the kind of driver who's ready to step on the brake if some idiot pulls in front of him unexpectedly.

"Are you sure you're talking about Oliver Doyle?" she asks nervously.

Keith gives a solemn nod. "I'm certain. I was with your husband, and before he lost consciousness he asked for Annie."

Annie's heart starts to hammer against her chest. She has a million questions, but the only thing she asks is, "How bad is it?" What she wants to know is, will Oliver live? But to ask that takes courage, the kind of courage she doesn't have right now.

"I think you'll want to be there," Keith says. "Mercy is a good hospital, and I'm sure they'll do whatever they can..." He stops there and leaves the remainder of the thought unsaid.

Annie is about to follow them back to the hospital when Max

screeches to a stop in the driveway. She jumps out of the car, rushes over to Annie and clasps her in an embrace.

"I heard," Max says.

WHEN ANNIE AND MAX ARRIVE at the hospital, Oliver has already been taken to the operating room. They are told to have a seat in the waiting room, and Doctor Sharma will speak with them as soon as he has something to report.

"Can't you just tell me how he is?" Annie asks.

The nurse shakes her head. "Sorry. You'll have to talk to Doctor Sharma."

Annie sits in the grey plastic chair beside Max, and they begin the long wait. At first the room swarms with anxiety: a crying baby, a bloody hand wrapped in a dishtowel, an elderly man doubled over in pain. All of them waiting. Frightened of what the diagnosis will be. The waiting, Annie knows, is often worse than the injury.

"How much longer?" the old man says, moaning. "I can't take the pain." A few minutes later he is taken back to an exam room. After him, the bloody hand disappears. One by one the emergency room seats empty out, and by midnight only Annie and Max are left sitting in the cavernous room.

Annie again goes to the desk to ask about Oliver.

"Does Doctor Sharma know I'm waiting to speak to him?" she asks.

The nurse has a look of intolerance. It has been a long day, and the weariness of it is written on her face.

"Yes, he knows." Her answer seems short and abrupt.

"Well, is there anyone else?" Annie asks. "Someone who can give me an update on how my husband is doing?"

"Only Doctor Sharma, and he's still in surgery."

Annie returns to her seat and clutches Max's hand. "If only they'd tell me something…"

Max wants to say something encouraging, but there is nothing to say. Not knowing is a hell of its own. The uncertainty tugs at them and begs them to ask again. It whispers this time there will be good news. This time the answer will be he's resting comfortably and they can now see him. So they ask again and again, but still there is only the ugliness of uncertainty.

After what seems like an eternity of waiting the nurse calls for Annie and tells her to go to the reception lounge on the second floor. She waggles a finger toward the hallway.

"Take the first elevator on the left," she says. "Doctor Sharma will join you there shortly."

Annie asks if she has word of Oliver's condition.

Nothing changes. She again shakes her head and replies, "I can't say. You'll have to—"

"I know," Annie cuts in. "Talk to Doctor Sharma."

THE SECOND FLOOR LOUNGE HAS the appearance of an ordinary living room. The smell of fresh-perked coffee comes from the pot on the corner table. The glaring overheads and bolted-down chairs of the emergency room are replaced with shaded lamps, cushioned sofas and carpeting. On the wall is a still life of flowers; beneath it a brass plaque reads "In memory of Benjamin Thurgood."

Max and Annie sit next to one another on the sofa. They are the only ones in the room.

"This doesn't look good," Annie says nervously.

"Why do you say that?" Max asks.

Annie gives a fearful looking shrug. "I can feel there's a lot of sorrow in this room."

"Nonsense," Max says, but the truth is she also has that feeling.

IT IS A HALF-HOUR wait before the dark-eyed doctor arrives. Rahul Sharma has a gentle manner but the face of a boy. Even before he has introduced himself, Annie starts to worry he is too young. Too young to have Oliver's life in his hands.

"Oliver…" she says fearfully. "Is he…"

Doctor Sharma raises his palm. "Not to worry."

He sits in the chair next to Annie. "Your husband is a lucky man. He is alive because they got him here so quickly."

"Thank God," Annie says with a loud exhale.

"Indeed." Sharma nods.

As he details Oliver's condition to Annie, his words are wise and his expression compassionate.

"When you see your husband, his head will be very swollen," he warns. "But I am hopeful that, given time, this swelling will go down and he will regain consciousness."

He explains the accident caused an epidural hematoma.

"Mister Doyle had blood leaking into the area of the brain," he says, "so we had to surgically create openings to alleviate the pressure." He deliberately does not say "drilled holes in Oliver's skull" because, although it was a life-saving necessity, the sound of such an action is harsh and difficult to understand.

Annie's eyes never leave Doctor Sharma's face as he speaks. She listens to every word, then tries to pick through them. Hopeful—Dr. Sharma said he was *hopeful,* yes—this is a word to keep, but there are so few others.

"Oliver has additional problems but none as serious as this," Sharma says. "The broken sternum is indeed painful, but with time and rest it will heal itself. The leg will need a second surgery and to be in a cast for maybe two months, but, again, this is not a worry."

As he slowly goes through the challenges facing a comatose patient, Annie realizes there is a painful truth hiding behind his words. Oliver may never wake up.

It is a thin line that separates living and dying, a line held in place by a single word: hopeful.

Her head drops into her lap and the tears come.

"No," she says through her sobs. "This can't be...no, please, no..."

Max wraps her arm around Annie's shoulders and hugs her closer.

"It is too soon for tears," Doctor Sharma says. "It is not good to waste yourself on tears while there is hope. Sorrow is the enemy of hope."

Annie lifts her head and looks into his face. "Please tell me the truth," she begs. Although she asks for truth, what she actually wants is reassurance, reassurance that her husband will live. She hesitates a moment then asks, "Is Oliver going to be okay?"

Without changing expression, he nods. "Yes, I believe there is a reasonably good chance. If Mister Doyle regains consciousness within the week, it is quite probable that he will make a full recovery."

"What if it's longer than a week?" Max asks cautiously.

Sharma gives his head a shake that is barely perceptible.

"Not as good," he says. "Eight days, yes, nine days, yes, but the longer a patient is in a coma, the less likely they will make a full recovery."

"Will Oliver know I'm there with him?" Annie asks.

Doctor Sharma tips his head; it is neither a yes nor a no. "That question medical science has yet to answer," he says "Some say yes, some say no. I believe when a bond is strong enough, anything is possible."

When he stands, Annie stands also. They shake hands, and she tearfully thanks him for all he has done for Oliver.

AFTER HE IS GONE, MAX wraps her arm around Annie.

"Don't worry," she says.

Such a request is like asking a mountain to rise up and dance.

ANNIE

Yesterday I could see the years of my life stretched out in front of me like a solid gold runway. Now I wonder if I'll make it through another day.

Poor Oliver looks worse than I could have ever dreamed. His head is one-and-a-half times what it should be, and the skin across his face is stretched so tight it looks paper-thin. He doesn't even blink an eye, just lies there and lets the machine do the breathing for him.

I don't know if he can hear me or not, but I keep talking to him. I tell him how much I love him, and I say when he gets better we're going to take that honeymoon we missed. I talk about all the places we'll go and the things we'll see, but the whole while I'm talking I'm praying maybe he will open one eye.

I won't let myself think about the possibility he won't wake up. Doing that would be the same as giving up. Oliver would never give up on me, and I'm not going to give up on him.

I asked Max to pray for us both. I know Max is not a praying person, but she said she would.

For Max that's the same as saying she loves us.

Day One

Oliver is now in the ICU ward. His room is a tiny square with machines on both sides of the bed and space enough for two small chairs. A few steps away there is a nurse's station. Someone is always at the desk.

The ICU is a place where death can happen in a heartbeat. There are no specified visiting hours. Family members can come and go at any hour of the day or night, and they can stay as long as they want. No nurse is willing to say go home when a loved one might breathe their last within the next few minutes.

Annie stands beside the bed holding Oliver's hand, touching his cheek, bending to kiss him. The face she touches is not the one she has etched in her mind. This face is oddly misshapen and covered with darkening bruises. But she sees beyond that; she sees Oliver as he has always been. She tells herself this is a temporary thing. In a day, maybe two, the swelling will go down and he will open his eyes. She whispers in his ear that soon this will be over, and one day they will be able to look back, breathe a sigh of relief and thank God for having made it through such a horrendous ordeal.

One day. Perhaps. Again and again the word "hopefully" comes to mind.

When her legs grow so weary she can no longer stand, Annie pulls the metal chair alongside the bed and sits. Still she holds his hand.

Max has been there throughout the night, but when morning comes she says she is going home to shower and grab a bite to eat.

"I'll be back in a few hours," she tells Annie. "Call me on my cell if you need anything."

"Take your time," Annie replies. "I'll be fine."

She glances at her watch. Eight-thirty. It is time to make some phone calls.

Annie's first call is to Oliver's parents. The telephone rings twice; then Ethan Allen answers. His caller ID tells him this is Annie calling from her cell.

"Getting the day off to an early start?" he says laughingly.

Annie thought she had the words ready, but the warmth of his laugh stops her.

"Hi, Dad," she says.

Ethan has insisted that she call him Dad just as Oliver does. "We're family," he'd said.

"Dad, I'm so, so sorry to have to tell you this..." Annie stumbles through an explanation of what has happened. She details Oliver's injuries just as Doctor Sharma has detailed them to her.

"Did he say what the prognosis is?" Ethan asks.

She repeats Doctor Sharma's explanation, word for word. "With brain trauma there's no guarantee of anything," she says. "They can't determine the degree of damage or even if there is any until Oliver regains consciousness and can speak."

Laura, Oliver's mom is on the extension. "Oh my God," she gasps.

A number of questions follow: how does Oliver look? Has he

been at all responsive? How are you holding up? Is this doctor any good?

The only question that has a positive answer is that of the doctor.

"He's great," Annie says. "He was here at seven this morning checking on Oliver."

"But is he capable?" Laura asks.

"Very," Annie answers. "He probably saved Oliver's life."

"You shouldn't have to go through this alone," Ethan says. "We're coming up there to be with you."

Annie is tempted to say there is no need, but the thought of having Oliver's parents with her is comforting so she says she is glad they are coming.

The next telephone call is to Charlie, Oliver's brother. It is barely five-thirty in California and when he answers the sound of sleep is still in his voice. Annie repeats what she has told his parents.

"I can be on the next plane," Charlie says.

"No," Annie answers. "There's nothing you can do right now. All anyone can do is wait and pray."

Oliver is Charlie's older brother, the rock he has always leaned on. The thought of losing him is is more than Charlie can bear. "There must be something…" he says sorrowfully.

Behind his words Annie hears the sound of a sob. "Don't worry," she says although she realizes such a thing is impossible. "As soon as I know something more, I'll text you," she promises.

"Call me," Charlie replies. "Call me if you need anything, anything at all."

ANNIE'S THIRD CALL IS TO Ophelia. This one is perhaps harder even than the call to Oliver's parents. Ophelia asks many of the same questions and Annie gives many of the same answers, but with Ophelia Annie drops the pretense of bravery.

"I'm scared to death," she says. "I keep talking to myself and trying to think positive thoughts, but when I see Oliver like this I can't help wondering what if he never wakes up?"

This time Annie cannot stop the tears. "It isn't fair. Our life was perfect; then in a split second some idiot driver takes it all away."

"I know," Ophelia says. "I know."

The truth is she does know. She remembers only too well the horrible days following Edward's death. She waits until Annie's sobbing subsides, then offers a word of advice.

"You're better off than I was," she says. "Oliver is alive and breathing. As long as there is breath in his body, there's hope." Although she thinks of it, she does not say with Edward there was no such hope; he was gone when she got there.

"You've got a gift," Ophelia says, "and now is the time to use it. If you can reach inside a rusty old bicycle and pull memories from it, you can surely do the same with Oliver. Don't let go of him, Annie. Find the right memories, and you'll be able to pull him back to you."

"But how will finding—"

"The memory of the accident is probably stuck in his subconscious. It's blocking everything else. You've got to find a memory powerful enough to push that one aside."

"What if he can't hear me? What if he doesn't even know I'm here?"

"Did the bicycle hear you?" Before Annie can argue the point, Ophelia answers her own question. "You know damn well it didn't. It was nothing but a rusty pile of junk. You gave it life, and you can do the same with Oliver."

WHEN THEY HANG UP, OPHELIA'S words remain in Annie's head. She pictures the bicycle and remembers how she spent endless weeks scraping the rust from it, polishing the fenders, banging the wheel back into shape. Even when she wasn't working on the bicycle she was thinking of it. The first time she touched it, she knew it was something special.

She also remembers the night she knocked on Oliver's door. The first time he smiled at her she knew he also was something special. It was a magic moment. A moment more vivid than all of the others in her memory. A moment that is forever locked in her mind. Surely it has to be the same for Oliver.

ANNIE TURNS BACK TO THE bed and leans across Oliver's body. She takes both of his hands in hers and touches her chest to his. "Remember the night we first met…" she whispers.

When Max returns early that afternoon Annie is still in the same position, but she has moved on to talking about all the things they've shared. She can feel Oliver's heartbeat and is determined not to let him go.

"I CAN STAY HERE WITH HIM while you take a break," Max suggests.

Annie shakes her head. "I'm not going to leave him."

"Don't you want to shower and maybe take a quick nap?"

Again Annie shakes her head. "I'll have time for those things after Oliver is well."

"Annie!" Max gives a reprimanding glare. "You've got to take care of yourself. You won't be any good to—"

"I'm not leaving here until Oliver regains consciousness," Annie says.

"It could be days, weeks, months even!"

"It won't be," Annie replies. "But if that's how long it takes, then that's how long I'll stay."

apologetically, "but I thought if I can make Oliver recall the good memories, he'll be able to move past this bad one."

"Not foolish at all," Sharma says. "At the foot of my baba, I learned memories are food of the soul."

"Really?"

"Yes, and from Maa I learned one must also have food to nourish the body." He gives an admonishing grin and asks, "Have you eaten today?"

Annie admits she hasn't.

There is the whisper of a tsk-tsk, then like Max he says she must take care of herself if she is to be strong enough to care for Oliver.

After he has looked in Oliver's blank eyes and tested his non-existent reflexes, Doctor Sharma reluctantly says, "Perhaps tomorrow."

As he leaves he gives Annie a nod and wishes her a restful evening.

Annie returns the nod. "You too."

She has come to like the way he nods. It is less than a hug but more than a handshake.

IT IS ALMOST AN HOUR after Doctor Sharma is gone when an aid comes to the room with dinner on a tray.

"I think you must be mistaken," Annie says. "Oliver is on a feeding tube."

"This isn't for him, it's for you."

"Me?"

The aid clears a spot on the table and sets the tray down. "It's from the staff cafeteria. Doctor Sharma said you should eat."

For the first time in what seems a thousand years, Annie smiles.

"Please thank him for me," she says.

AS EVENING SLIPS INTO NIGHT, the ICU grows increasingly quiet. The phones stop ringing, the endless stream of visitors disappears and only two nurses are left on duty. One of them is settled at the desk with a book in hand.

It is a peaceful silence, one that masks the frantic pace of the daylight hours. Annie listens to the soft hum of monitors and the steady whoosh of Oliver's breathing machine. These are the sounds of life. Earlier she could feel his heartbeat, but now she can hear it as well. In the stillness of night, even the tiniest sound is magnified.

Annie bends over the bed and puts her ear against his chest. She listens to the thump, thump, thump of his heart. It comes in measured beats, steady and even. He is alive and trapped inside his body. She touches her hands to his face, then traces her fingers along the curve of his cheek. She moves her fingertips to his eyelids, her touch barely more than the tickle of a feather.

"Remember our wedding night?" she says. "When you touched me, I knew there would never be another love such as ours."

She bends lower and puts her lips to his ear.

"You promised no matter what life had in store for us you'd never stop loving me," she whispers. "Love me now. Please, Oliver, love me now. Love me enough to fight your way back."

Tears fall from Annie's eyes and slide down Oliver's swollen cheek.

Suddenly she feels the beat of his heart growing faster. She lifts her head and looks at his face. It is still as it was. His eyes remain closed, and there is not even a flinch of muscle.

Seconds later Phyllis, the night nurse, comes hurrying in with a look of alarm tugging at her face.

"What happened?" she asks.

Annie shrugs. "Nothing as far as I know."

"Nothing?" Phyllis repeats. "That's strange." She checks the various monitor connections and feels for Oliver's pulse. "You sure he didn't open his eyes or make some small movement? Maybe when you weren't watching?"

"I'm positive," Annie says. "I was looking at him the whole time."

Phyllis shakes her head as if this is a puzzle that eludes her. "I could have sworn..."

"Sworn what?" Annie asks.

"There was turbulence in his heart rate. Something like that usually happens when the patient is stimulated. It's like an adrenalin rush."

"I was talking to him," Annie says. "Could it be—"

Phyllis shrugs. "That's not usually enough to stimulate the patient, but stranger things have happened." She turns to leave then looks back. "I'm going to ask Doctor Sharma about physical therapy. I think that might help."

Annie smiles. It was nothing but a rapid heartbeat, but she wants to believe it was an answer.

THE GOOD DOCTOR

It is an acknowledged fact that Rahul Sharma is the first doctor to arrive each morning and the last to leave each evening. It has been this way since he became the head of neurology five years earlier. When he arrives at six-thirty the next morning, Phyllis catches him before he gets to Oliver's room.

"I'm not sure if this qualifies as progress or not," she says and explains Oliver's rapid heartbeat. "The duration was only forty seconds, but he went from 89 to 162. The wife said all she did was talk to him, but I'm thinking maybe physical therapy—"

Sharma smiles. "Good observation," he says and turns into Oliver's room.

THE SMALL STRAIGHT-BACKED CHAIR is close to the bed. Annie sits there with her head tilted onto her shoulder and Oliver's hand clasped in hers. She is dozing. Last night's dinner tray is still on the table. The soup bowl is empty and half a sandwich is gone. Sharma smiles, then touches his hand to her arm.

Annie wakes with a start.

"I must have fallen asleep," she says. As she pulls herself up, she feels a kink in her neck and groans then rolls her head to loosen the stiffness.

Sharma gives a polite smile. "You remained here all night?"

Annie nods. "Yes, and thank you for the dinner. I really appreciate it."

"You are most welcome." He nods.

He goes to Oliver and starts his examination. Again he waves the tiny flashlight back and forth in front of Oliver's eyes; still there is no reaction. He then takes Oliver's arm, lifts it into a bended position and straightens it. He repeats this motion with the other arm and the leg that is not in a cast.

He then turns to Annie. "I would normally chastise you for not going home to have proper rest." A slight smile curls the corner of his mouth. "But it appears you may have done some good here."

He explains that while a quickening of the heart can be nothing but an involuntary muscle spasm, it can also be an indication of awareness.

"Awareness is the first step to consciousness," he says. "A baby step at most, but better than nothing."

Annie gives a broad smile. She sees this tiny bit of hope as huge.

"That means Oliver heard me," she says.

"That is only a possibility," Doctor Sharma warns. He knows he should impress upon Annie this is only a remote possibility, but perhaps he also wants to believe her faith can move mountains.

ETHAN ALLEN AND LAURA ARRIVE shortly before noon. They rent a car and come straight from the airport. Laura's eyes are red and puffy. It is obvious she has been crying. She is first into Oliver's room.

The moment she sees him, her hand flies to her mouth and she muffles a gasp. Her eyes fall on Annie and she says, "I didn't realize he'd look so—"

Annie puts her finger to her lips and gives a soft hushing sound. She motions to Oliver then mouths the words, "He can hear what you say."

Laura gives a knowing nod, then leans over Oliver and kisses his cheek. "Mommy's here, sweetheart," she says. Although she tries to give her words a lighter sound, her voice is nasal and clogged with pushed back tears.

Ethan comes and stands beside her. He wraps his arm around Laura. When he speaks his voice is level; it has no telltale sign of sorrow but the sorrow is there. It is in his eyes and steely set of his jaw.

"Annie tells us you're getting the best of care," he says. "That's good." He hesitates and lets his eyes come to rest on Oliver's face. "I know this is one shitty battle you're fighting; but, son, you're a Doyle, and Doyle men are tough."

He swallows, trying to rid himself of the lump in his throat, then bends and kisses Oliver. There is so much more he wants to say, but he can't get past his grief long enough to say it.

Annie motions for Laura and Ethan to follow her. They step outside the room and the moment they are beyond hearing range, Laura breaks into loud sniffling sobs.

"I'm sorry," she says, "I just wasn't ready for—"

"None of us were," Annie says.

She explains her theory of using memories to open up a pathway through Oliver's blocked subconscious.

"We don't know what's in his mind right now," she says. "But we know what was there. All that stuff is still in there, we just have to make him remember it."

"Sounds like it could be worth a try," Ethan says.

"Oh, it definitely is." Annie tells them what happened last night. "I'm almost positive he heard what I was saying but couldn't break through that block in his subconscious."

Laura dabs her eyes then asks, "So you think remembering his life will bring him out of this coma?"

"Yes, I do." Annie nods. "The problem is I only know his memories of this past year." She looks at Ethan. "You know the story of his entire life."

Laura turns to Ethan.

"You should be the one," she says. "Oliver's always been so close to you. You'll know how to get inside his head and see things the way he'd see them." She gives a bittersweet smile and says, "I'm his mama and I'll be his mama until the day I die, but you're the influencer in his life."

THAT AFTERNOON, LAURA TAKES THE rented car and goes to Memory House. She and Ethan will stay there for now.

Ethan remains at the hospital and spends the afternoon talking to Oliver. He speaks of college years, law school, the days of being a lawyer and the day Oliver received his appointment as a judge.

"I can't imagine any daddy being more proud of his boy than I was of you that day," he says. His words are soft, gentle and filled with the sweetness of memory.

In his eyes, however, Annie can see the sadness of loss. It is there, just as it is in her heart. In time the weariness can be heard in his voice. The memories, regardless of how sweet, are like drops of water falling on stone; in time they wear away his resolve.

"You look tired," she tells him.

"You too," Ethan replies.

This brief moment of conversation is interrupted when a young man in scrubs taps on the frame of the door.

"Physical therapy," he announces, then walks in.

"I think you have the wrong room," Annie says.

He glances down at the clipboard. "This Oliver Doyle?"

"Yes, but..."

"Oliver Doyle," he says, "that's right."

He moves to the bed, pulls back the sheet covering Oliver, then turns to Annie and Ethan. "This is gonna take thirty-forty minutes; you can go for coffee if you want."

The expression on Annie's face is one of outrage. "Are you out of your mind? Can't you see my husband is comatose?"

"Of course I see," he says. "That's why he's getting therapy."

"Is it supposed to bring him out of the coma?" Ethan asks.

The therapist lifts Oliver's right arm and starts to bend it back and forth. "No. But it helps with muscle atrophy. Rehab's a lot easier for patients who have had ongoing therapy."

"Did Doctor Sharma order this?" Annie asks.

"Yep," the therapist answers and moves to bending Oliver's wrist back and forth.

Annie smiles and tugs Ethan Allen out of the room.

"You know what this means?" she whispers.

Ethan gives her a puzzled look. "Not exactly."

"It means Doctor Sharma believes Oliver is going to get well," she says. "He's looking down the road at rehabilitation."

WHILE THE THERAPIST WORKS WITH Oliver, Annie and the man she now calls Dad walk down the hallway together. They go into the sunroom at the end of the corridor. On the table there is a pot of coffee with paper cups stacked next to it.

"Can I buy you a cup of coffee?" Ethan says with a laugh.

"That would be nice," Annie replies.

He has his black; she has hers with powdered milk and imitation sugar because that's all that is there. She wrinkles her nose. "Not nearly as good as my dandelion tea."

"I'll stay with Oliver," Ethan volunteers. "You go home and get some rest."

Annie shakes her head. "No, thanks. I'm staying here until Oliver regains consciousness. I'm not going to take a chance on him opening his eyes and not seeing me there."

Ethan puts his arm around Annie and gives her a hug. "Oliver's lucky to have you."

"I'm lucky to have him too," she replies. "Some day when this is all over we'll look back and..." Her voice trails off. Laugh is the wrong word. They'll never laugh about it. Cry, perhaps, but by then it will be over, so there will no longer be a reason to cry.

Finally she thinks of the right words.

"We'll thank God we've survived," she says.

"Amen to that," Ethan says.

WHEN THEY HAVE FINISHED THEIR coffee, they walk back to the room. The therapist is still working with Oliver.

"It's late," Annie tells Ethan. "Go back to the house and stay with Mom."

Ethan tries to convince Annie she is the one who needs rest, but she refuses to leave.

"It's very quiet here at night," she says. "It's a good time for me to be alone with Oliver."

No amount of insistence changes her mind, so in the end Ethan goes and leaves her to spend another night sitting beside Oliver.

AT SEVEN-THIRTY DOCTOR SHARMA comes for his final check on Oliver.

As he prods the skin of Oliver's cheeks, he says, "Ah, less edema. This is good."

"Does that mean Oliver is getting better?" Annie asks.

"It means the pressure on the brain is less," Sharma says. "Getting better I save for when he is awake."

Annie smiles. "You believe like I do, that Oliver is going to get better, don't you?"

Rahul Sharma has a serious face, and despite the goodness of his heart he seldom has the look of a happy man. The corners of his mouth take on an almost imperceptible curl.

"I cannot know if this is true or not true," he says, "but I can tell you the unselfish love such as you have for Mister Doyle deserves reward."

He gives his customary nod and leaves.

A SHORT WHILE LATER ANNIE'S dinner is again delivered on a tray. And later that evening two porters bring a lounge sleeper to the room. The nurse comes, and they rearrange the machines to make room for the chair.

THAT NIGHT ANNIE SLEEPS BESIDE Oliver with her hand closed around his.

LAURA DOYLE

I can't imagine a hell worse than seeing your child lying there more dead than alive. Any mother would say the same thing. It makes no difference whether he's three or thirty; he's still your baby. When I saw Oliver looking as he did, I could feel my heart break apart inside of me.

It wasn't easy to walk away and let Ethan be the one to stay. But when it comes to remembering the things that were important to Oliver, I knew his daddy would be the one who'd be best at it.

When Oliver was a boy he was practically tied to my apron strings, but once he got to be twelve or so he belonged to his daddy. Whatever Ethan did, Oliver wanted to do. It didn't matter if he was cleaning out the garage or watching a football game. If Ethan was going to the hardware store, Oliver would run behind saying, Wait up, Dad, I'll go with you.

If anyone has a memory that can bring Oliver back, it's Ethan.

Or perhaps Annie.

I know she loves Oliver as much as I do. When a man finds a woman who loves him as much as his mama did, then he's got himself a true treasure.

I don't know how Annie came up with this idea about giving Oliver back his memories, but it sounds reasonable enough.

One thing for sure is she's got an active imagination. Oliver once told me Annie finds memories in places where no one else would even think to look. I pray she'll find the memory that will bring Oliver back to life. If she does that I'll fall down and worship her for the rest of my days, so help me God I will.

THE ULTIMATUM

The day after the recliner is delivered, it is as if Annie herself has moved into the hospital. Doctor Sharma stops suggesting she go home to sleep and accepts that she will be there for the duration. Every afternoon a lunch tray is delivered to the room and every evening a dinner tray comes. There is no note, no explanation; only a ticket from the staff cafeteria with her name and Oliver's room number.

Annie can tell the writing on the ticket has the same crooked slant as Rahul Sharma's notes, but when she tries to thank him he shrugs and claims to have no knowledge of it.

Martha Macomb, the long-faced ICU nurse who works Monday through Friday, sees Sharma paying for the ticket with Annie's name on it. She scowls and says, "Why don't you just tell her you're the one sending her the meals?"

Sharma puts his finger to his lips as if this is something to be hushed.

"A good deed," he says, "is not a good deed if it is done with expectation of praise." He nods and walks away.

"Well, I'll be," Martha says in amazement.

Early the next morning Martha carries in a crocheted afghan

and surreptitiously slides it across the arm of Annie's chair. When the other nurses question where the afghan came from, Martha says nothing. That afternoon is the first and only time her fellow nurses have seen Martha looking quite so happy.

BEFORE THE WEEK IS OUT, everyone has established a routine of coming and going. Laura comes in the morning and visits. She reminds Oliver of his childhood: a red dump truck, his big wheel bicycle and rainy days of baking cookies together. When she speaks of these things her voice often falters and tears fall, but Oliver remains the same.

In the afternoon Ethan visits. He talks about the things they've shared: football games, fishing trips, camping expeditions.

"Remember that Thanksgiving we camped at Shenandoah Park? Remember how you and Charlie wanted to catch your own fish for dinner, and we ended up eating baloney sandwiches?"

The spark of remembering is obvious in the fondness of Ethan's words, but it does nothing to change Oliver.

Charlie calls every morning and again in the evening. He asks how Oliver is doing and when Annie says there has been no change she can hear the sorrow in his sigh. "I was hoping..." he says, but the words end there.

Max also checks in every day. She comes to visit but doesn't stay long, because the ICU allows only two visitors at a time and there are others who need to be with Oliver. Max has no real memories to contribute, but she is concerned about Annie.

"Call me if you need anything," she says. "Anything at all."

On Friday Annie does call.

"They said I can shower in the nurse's lounge," she tells Max. "Can you stop by the house and grab some clean clothes for me?"

"Sure," Max says. "No problem."

That same afternoon she brings a bag with clothes, toiletries and a jar of dandelion tea.

"I know how much you enjoy this, so I brewed a pot."

"You actually took time to brew a pot of tea?" Annie asks.

"This one time," Max laughs. "That's it. Don't expect I'll do it again."

Although she says this, the truth is Max would do anything in the world for Annie. Anything. Unfortunately there is nothing she or anyone else can do to change the way things are. Doing nothing is harder than anything Annie might ask for.

Ophelia also visits. She comes with the driver of the Baylor car. He waits in the lobby while she comes upstairs.

"I understand what you're going through," she tells Annie, "and my heart aches for you."

"Don't worry about me," Annie says. "It's Oliver we have to worry about."

ALTHOUGH ANNIE SAYS "DON'T WORRY about me," the truth is she looks almost as bad as Oliver. She dozes from time to time but seldom sleeps. Her eyes have gone from violet to the steely grey of Ophelia's. Sometimes she nibbles at the food on the dinner trays, but more often than not she pushes the plate back and leaves the meal untouched.

In the five days she has been here, Annie has shed a million tears. At night when the ward is silent the nurses hear her talking to Oliver, sometimes praying and sometimes reminding him of why he needs to live.

"Please, Oliver," she begs. "Please. Do you remember the day we were married? You can't possibly forget the church bells. Or the party. Remember those nights in the loft? You've got to come back, Oliver. All this is nothing without you. I'm nothing without you."

FRIDAY NIGHT IS THE FIFTH night. Annie has counted every minute, every hour and, perhaps most painful of all, every day. A week, Doctor Sharma said. A week, and then Oliver's chances of recovery grow slimmer.

This night Annie does not sleep at all. She holds his hand in hers, touches his face and whispers in his ear.

"Please don't give up," she says. "Please, Oliver. I'm going to stay here until you open your eyes and talk to me. I'm not going home. Not ever. Not until you come home with me."

She drops her head against his chest and lies there listening to his heartbeat. He is alive. He needs only to open his eyes.

"Please open your eyes," she begs. "Don't do this. The accident is over now. You're going to be okay. All you have to do is open your eyes. Please, Oliver, please…"

WHEN DOCTOR SHARMA ARRIVES SATURDAY morning, Annie is still lying in the same position. The sheet is soaked through with her tears.

"What's this?" he asks and gently lifts her head.

Annie's face is gaunt and her eyes swollen from the tears. She has the look of a woman who has been drained of life.

"This is not good," Sharma says. "Not good at all."

"I know," Annie says wearily. "It's five days."

Using his index finger Sharma tugs on Annie's cheek and looks at the inside rim of her left eye. "Not good," he repeats.

"I know it's not good." A tear overflows Annie's eye. "Can't you do something?"

"Yes," Sharma nods. "I can give you a pill for sleep and a nutritional supplement."

"Me? I'm not talking about me, I'm talking about Oliver!"

"Oliver will wake when he is ready," Sharma says. "There is nothing to change that. But you getting sick I can change."

"There's nothing wrong with—"

"You are dehydrated, and from the look of you I would say also malnourished. Do you not eat the food you are given?"

"Some," Annie says. She knows he has sent the food, and such an answer seems so ungrateful. "I'm sorry but I haven't had much of an appet—"

"I will make a deal with you," Sharma says. "You let me take a blood test to make certain you are okay, then I give you a pill for sleeping and you agree to eat the food you are sent. If these things happen, I will allow you to stay and be with Mister Doyle."

"*Allow* me to stay?" Annie's voice has a note of disbelief in it.

"Yes," Sharma says. "If you do not agree to these things, I will say there are to be no visitors."

"You wouldn't."

He gives a firm and unyielding nod. "I would."

Doctor Rahul Sharma

Perhaps I should keep my nose on my face, but I cannot stand by and see a nice girl like Annie make herself sick.

To become a doctor I vowed that I will do no harm. Is it not harm to see a person suffering and turn your eyes to another place? I say yes. If you do no harm, then you must do good.

To do good you give a kindness and expect no pay. For the business of healing you receive pay, but for a kindness you receive only the joy of knowing you have done good.

This is as The Holy One declared, and I obey.

Many people are sick, but their loved ones do not stay by their side as this Annie Doyle does. She is a person worthy of a good deed.

If you would say it is to muddle in someone else's business, then I would say I am sorry. But even if I say I am sorry, I would not do a different thing because I believe what I do is as it should be.

If this is to be called poking my face into another person's business, then so be it.

ANNIE'S DREAM

Given no choice, Annie agrees to Doctor Sharma's terms. That same morning he makes a second trip to Oliver's room. This time, he hands her two sample size bottles of vitamin B+ and a full size bottle of multivitamins.

"These you take two of," he tells her.

Annie frowns at the label. "It says one a day."

"For you it is two. It is one when I say one."

From someone else this might sound bossy or argumentative, but from Rahul Sharma it is not. His manner is gentle, and his expression that of a worried old woman.

Once Annie has swallowed the pills, she sits in the chair and allows him to draw a vial of blood.

"I'm sorry to be all this trouble," she says.

"This is not trouble for me," Sharma says. "Caring for sick people is my job, but so much worry is bad for you."

He looks at her with a furrowed brow. "Worry does not change anything. Worry makes people sick; then I have two sick people instead of one."

Annie gives him a sad smile. "It's hard not to worry when someone you love—"

"Did you not listen? Worry changes nothing."

"But you said if Oliver didn't wake up in a week, his chances—"

"No, no, no." Sharma waves his palm in the air. "I said it is *better* if he wakes up sooner."

"Oh." Annie gives a sigh of relief. "So even if it's longer than a week—"

"Some patients come back fast, an hour, a day, maybe two. Others take longer, but they are still okay." He doesn't mention that some never come out of a coma; this is something Annie doesn't need to hear. "Your Oliver will open his eyes when it is his time."

"Tomorrow it will be a week—"

"No matter," Sharma says. "But when it happens, he will need therapy. So you need to be strong enough to help him—"

"Oh, I will," Annie assures him. "I definitely will."

"A sick woman is not strong. If you are to be there for what your Oliver needs, you must eat food, take vitamins and sleep."

THAT AFTERNOON WHEN THE LUNCH tray arrives, Annie finishes everything. Although her stomach feels queasy at first, after she eats a slice of bread it is better. That in itself is rather odd, since plain white bread has always been something she turned her nose up at. Biscuits, anytime. Crusty rolls, yes. But plain white bread— almost never.

When the dinner tray arrives it is the same way. Annie eats the bread and then twenty minutes later has appetite enough for the remainder of the food.

That evening when Doctor Sharma makes his last visit of the day, he gives Annie a shot. It is a mild sedative, enough to make her sleep.

Shortly after eight o'clock the sound of soft snores can be heard coming from Oliver's room.

AS THE DAYS HAVE LUMBERED by Annie has listened to the stories of Oliver's life, each story taken from a memory so vivid she can imagine it as it was. When she finally drifts off to sleep, the images of what has been told come to her.

Oliver, a baby in the young Laura's arms.

In less than a heartbeat he is a toddler filling a dump truck with sand. Before she has had her fill of this vision, a gust of wind blows and the sand becomes a snowstorm. For a moment there is only white, but when the air clears Oliver is a teenager. A boy who is all arms and legs but with the smile she loves. He laughingly brings his hand from behind his back and offers out a bouquet of pink peonies. Annie recognizes the flowers; it is her wedding bouquet. She reaches out to take hold of it, and suddenly he is gone. Swallowed up by a crowd of people.

"Come back!" she screams, but no sound comes from her mouth.

Helplessly she wanders through the crowd until she at last comes upon Oliver. He is now dressed in a cap and gown. A graduation no doubt, but which one is not clear.

"Oliver," Annie calls out. "Oliver, I'm here!"

To him she is invisible and without sound.

If she can only touch him... Annie tries to move, but her feet seem glued to the ground. Regardless of how she tugs and pulls, she cannot free herself. When she bends to loosen her feet from her shoes, she hears the sound of laughter.

"It's too soon," a voice says.

Annie lifts her head and looks behind her. No one is there. When she glances back Oliver is gone.

"I told you," the voice says. "It is too soon!"

"If it's too soon," she screams, "then take me to the right time and place! Take me to where—"

Again a rush of air swirls around her. It is thick and hard like sand or sleet. It lifts her from the ground, and there is no longer anything to hold on to. No hand to grab, no earth beneath her feet. Annie covers her eyes, and when she reopens them she is on an unfamiliar street.

Across from where she stands there is a courthouse. Two figures stand on the steps. She moves closer. It is Oliver and his daddy. Ethan's hair is just starting to gray at the temples, and Oliver looks younger than he did the day she met him.

She calls out, but there is no sound to her words. She can do nothing other than stand and watch.

Ethan gives his son the book he is holding. Oliver looks at the inside page, then smiles and wraps his arms around his father.

Annie moves closer. She wants to see the book and hear what they are saying. As she steps out to cross the street there is a loud crash. The sound of glass shattering, the clang of metal...

Annie wakes with a start.

"I'm so sorry," the aid says, "I came to pick up your tray, and it slid from my hand." She scrambles to her knees retrieving pieces of the broken dinner plate and setting the metal wastebasket back on its feet.

"That's okay," Annie says. "Accidents happen."

She scoots from her chair and bends to help the girl, but as she reaches down the floor comes up to meet her. That's the last thing Annie remembers.

WHEN SHE COMES TO, A perturbed-looking Phyllis stands over her.

"Dehydration," she growls. "Just look at this." She pinches

Annie's arm and the wrinkles remain. "When the skin doesn't bounce back that's a sure sign."

She hands Annie a bottle of Gatorade. "Drink."

Annie downs several swallows, then says, "I had a dream—"

"It was no dream," Phyllis says. "You fainted."

"Before that," Annie says. She wants to explain the dream but doesn't herself understand it.

THE BOOK

After everything has again quieted down, Annie stands beside Oliver's bed and holds his hand.

"Please, Oliver," she says wearily. "Please tell me what memory is powerful enough to make you fight your way back into this world."

There is no answer, just the whoosh of the breathing machine and the occasional beep of a monitor.

Annie thinks back to the day she first came to Memory House. Back then she laughed at the thought of a memory attached to anything. Of course, that was before she discovered the bicycle. It was before she found the book that led her to...

The book.

"That's it!" she shouts. "It's the book!"

Phyllis comes running in. "Are you alright?"

Annie grabs Phyllis and dances her around. "It's the book!"

"What's wrong with you?" Phyllis asks and wriggles free.

"The book is Oliver's most powerful memory," Annie says. "He told me the proudest moment of his life was the day he was sworn in as a judge. That's when his daddy gave him the book dedicated to him."

"I don't see what—"

Annie doesn't even slow down. "Don't you see? That was Oliver's proudest moment, but his happiest moment was when I showed up at his door."

"I still don't get it," Phyllis says.

"The book is what brought me there. I found it when I was working at the library, and the minute I touched it I knew Ethan Allen Doyle was the bicycle boy I'd been searching for."

"Ethan Allen? Oliver's daddy?"

"Yes." Annie nods. "Ethan Allen wrote that book, and it has powerful memories stuck to it. It brought Oliver and me together, and now it's going to bring him out of this coma."

Phyllis eyes Annie with a worried look. "Maybe that sedative was a bit too strong."

Annie laughs, and this time her laughter has a tinge of happiness attached to it. Even though it is one o'clock in the morning, she pulls out her cell phone and punches in the number for Memory House.

LAURA AND ETHAN ARE ALREADY in bed, but neither of them is sleeping. Sleep is difficult to come by these days. Like Annie they spend endless hours thinking about Oliver.

Laura is his mother; she worries as any mother would worry. Ethan frets because he has no idea of how to make things better. It is a father's job to fix things, he tells himself, yet this is something he cannot fix.

When the telephone jangles in the dead of night, Laura clutches her heart. "Oh, dear God," she says. "Please don't tell me..."

Ethan pushes himself from the bed and hurries to the telephone. He answers with a tentative, "Hello."

"I figured it out," Annie says. The words come so quickly they bump up against each other, and Ethan has to ask her to repeat what she's said.

She tells him the same story she has told Phyllis.

"The book is what ties everything together. It gave Oliver his proudest and happiest moment," she says.

Ethan looks at Laura, signals that there is no emergency, then asks, "What book?"

"The Wisdom of Judicial Judgment in the Practice of Law."

He thinks back and catches the image of that day standing on the courthouse steps. "And you think that's it?"

"I'm almost positive," Annie replies.

She tells him Oliver's copy of the book is on the bookshelf in the loft. "Second shelf on the right hand side. Would you get it and bring it to me?"

"Now?" he asks.

"The sooner the better," Annie says. "I'm anxious to get started."

ONCE ANNIE HAS THE BOOK, she rests it on the side of the bed and moves Oliver's hand onto the open cover. She turns to the first page and starts to read.

"This book is dedicated to my son, the Honorable Oliver E. Doyle, Judge, Eastern District Court of Virginia."

Annie turns the page and continues reading. "The mission of the Judicial System is to insure that disputes are resolved justly, promptly and economically. The components necessary to discharge this function constitute a court system unified in its structure and administration, competent, honest judges and court personnel, a court with uniform rules of practice and procedure..."

Annie reads until the sun crosses the horizon. The rays of light dancing across the page eventually tire her eyes, and she drifts off to sleep.

⊗ß

TODAY IS SUNDAY, THE DAY when Doctor Sharma visits the hospital just once in the afternoon. When he arrives Annie is sound asleep. He slides the book from beneath her hands and places it on the table. Although she doesn't wake, Oliver's right eyelid flutters.

It is barely a movement. A flutter so small it could easily go unnoticed by an unskilled eye. Sharma waits and watches. He remains there for a half hour and when there is nothing more, he turns to leave.

The sun is high in the sky, so the shadow of his movement falls across Annie's face and wakes her.

She stretches and yawns. "I was reading to Oliver and must have fallen asleep. Have you been here long?"

"Only a few moments," he says. He makes no mention of the fluttering eyelid because it could be nothing. And if it is something, he wants Annie to have the joy of claiming it. "Is there anything new to report?"

"Well, I'm feeling a bit better today," Annie says. "If I eat a slice of bread before dinner, my tummy is a lot less queasy."

"Interesting," Sharma says and nods. "And with Mister Doyle, any changes?"

"Not yet," Annie says. "But I think maybe today."

There is a strange new sound of confidence in her voice. It piques Sharma's curiosity. "Why today?"

"I think I've found something powerful enough to pull him out of this coma." She smiles and taps her finger on the book. "It's this."

199

Sharma angles his head sideways and reads the title. "The Wisdom of Judicial Judgment in the Practice of Law."

Annie grins. "It's Oliver's favorite book." She lifts it from the table, turns to the opening page and hands it to him. "See, it's dedicated to Oliver."

"Interesting." Sharma holds the book open and scans a few pages. It is like the medical textbooks he studied: words, words, words piled one on top of the other. Sentences so long they became a paragraph.

Thinking back on those tedious hours of reading, he asks, "Do you think a different type of story might be more stimulating? A story of love, perhaps?"

Annie shakes her head. "Nothing could be more special than this book; it was written by his father. It's the thread that ties everything together."

THROUGHOUT THE AFTERNOON ANNIE READS to Oliver. They are long sentences with cumbersome words that stumble across her tongue—amicus curiae, de facto, exculpatory, habeas corpus. She is on page 48 when she looks up and sees his eyes are open.

"Oliver!" she screams.

The book falls to the floor as she jumps up and leans over him.

"Thank God, you're alright," she says. "I've been praying night and day..."

Suddenly she notices he is not looking at her. His eyes are open, but they seem to see nothing.

"Do you know who I am?" she asks.

His eyes follow the sound and shift slightly to the right where she stands, but there is no other response.

"Oliver, it's me. Annie!" There is a new desperation in her

voice. "Do you know where you are? Do you remember the accident?"

He looks in her direction a few seconds longer, then closes his eyes again.

Annie calls out for the nurse. "Something's wrong. Oliver opened his eyes but then closed them again."

"That can happen," the nurse replies. "It may be the start of him coming out of the coma."

Annie's eyes are now filled with tears. "You don't understand. He didn't even know who I was."

The nurse gives Annie's shoulders a squeeze of reassurance. "Don't worry. Most of the time they get back to remembering, sooner or later."

Most of the time? Sooner or later?

The thought keeps racing through Annie's mind. *He was awake but didn't know me.* She cannot help but wonder if this accident will have wiped away all his memories. Her. His family. This book.

It is a long while before Annie picks up the book and begins to read again. This time it is with greater purpose. In between the sentences of legalese, she adds stories of their life. A mention of the wedding. A reference to Max's plan for the added wing. Memory House. The loft. The nights they spent lying on a blanket beneath the stars. The time they made love beneath the weeping willow.

In the wee hours of the morning, Annie's words drift off and she falls asleep. When the book falls to the floor, Oliver's foot twitches. Annie doesn't see this because her eyes are already closed.

THE FIRST WORD

On Monday morning when the lab opens at seven, Doctor Sharma is already waiting at the door. Before the attendant switches on the overhead light, Sharma asks for the report on Annie Doyle.

"Let me check if it's ready," the attendant says and disappears into the back.

It is fifteen minutes before he reappears with the report. "Looks like you're gonna have a happy patient," he says then hands the report to Sharma.

It is as Rahul suspected. Annie is pregnant. Given the circumstances, he is uncertain whether this will be good news or bad.

WHEN ANNIE WAKES SHE GLANCES at the clock. Seven-ten.

"Oh dear," she says, "I hope I haven't missed Doctor Sharma."

This, of all mornings, she needs to talk with him. She needs to tell him of the changes. Even more so, she needs to hear him say Oliver's blank stare is normal; that given time he will remember her and the life they have together.

If it takes a year or ten years, Annie is determined to make it happen. The book caused Oliver to open his eyes so she will continue to read from it, even if she has to read and then reread all nine hundred and eighty-seven pages.

She squats next to the bed and stretches her arm to reach the book where it has slid under the bed. Her shoulder pushes against the bed and jostles Oliver.

He opens his eyes again and senses the tube taped to his mouth. He wants to reach up and yank it from his lips, but his arms don't move. His mouth twitches to the right, and his jaw moves.

Once Annie has pulled the book from beneath the bed, she sits in the chair with it in her lap and opens it to page eighty-three. This is where she left off. Before she starts to read she looks across at Oliver.

His eyes are again open, but this time there is a sense of panic in them.

Annie sets the book aside, steps to the bed and lifts his hand into hers. "Don't be frightened. Everything is going to be okay."

Her voice is soothing and comfortable, like a familiar song, but Oliver can only faintly remember where he has heard it before.

This time instead of asking questions, Annie gives answers.

"You're in Mercy General Hospital," she says. "There was a car accident..." She says nothing more about the accident, because it is something that could send him back into the painless world of not remembering.

"Your name is Oliver Doyle, and I'm your wife, Annie. We were married on June fifth at the Good Shepherd Church in Burnsville." She hesitates a moment then asks, "Do you remember any of that?"

He blinks his eyes, and Annie suspects he has also made an effort to nod. Although she does not see his head move, there is a distinct shift in the fabric of the pillowcase.

The words that follow are wrapped in a prayer bigger than anything Annie has ever asked for in all of her life. "Oliver, if you can understand what I am saying, squeeze my hand or blink twice."

For a moment there is nothing. Annie's hand holds his with a touch so light she can feel even the slightest twinge of movement. She watches his face and then, after what seems an eternity, he blinks twice.

"Thank you, God!" Annie shouts. "Thank you, thank you, thank you!"

Her shout is heard at the nurse's station, and Nancy Pearl comes running in. "Is there a problem?"

With a grin that stretches the full width of her face, Annie says, "Oliver is awake and alive!"

WHEN DOCTOR SHARMA ARRIVES AT eight-thirty, Annie is standing beside the bed telling Oliver stories of their life together. There is much he does not remember, but every so often he blinks an acknowledgment of something Annie has mentioned.

Sharma sees this. "Ah, it looks like our patient is finally awake."

"Not only awake! He understands what I am saying!"

Annie feels compelled to demonstrate this. "Blink twice to show Doctor Sharma."

He blinks twice.

"Very good." Sharma nods. "Any muscle movements?"

Oliver makes an effort to answer, but with the breathing tube taped to his mouth it is impossible. The muscle on the right side of his face twitches.

"Very good," Sharma repeats. "You have a breathing tube in because your sternum was fractured. It is now stabilized and you should be able to breathe on your own, so I am going to remove the tube from your throat. Is that okay?"

Oliver blinks twice.

Sharma goes to the sink, scrubs his hands, then returns to Oliver's bedside. As he works he talks, explaining each movement. He gently pries the edges of the adhesive tape from Oliver's skin.

"Removing the intubation will not hurt," he assures Oliver. "Once it is out you will feel much better. Your throat may be dry and scratchy for a few days, so drink plenty of water…"

He steps back, drops the used tubing into a disposal bag and says, "All done."

Oliver's first few gasps of air are labored, and he winces from the pain in his chest. Once the panic of the moment passes, he settles into a rhythmic pattern of shallow breaths.

"Better?" Sharma asks.

Oliver blinks twice.

As his chest rises and falls, Annie leans down, puts her lips to his and kisses him. That gentle kiss is a memory Oliver will hold onto for the rest of his days.

NOT ALL OF DOCTOR SHARMA'S patients are success stories. This one is, so he allows himself to stay and enjoy the moment. Happy though it may be, he knows there is still an uphill road ahead.

"Recovery is a slow process," he warns. "You may feel frustrated by words you can't remember or motor skills that seem too difficult, but you'll have physical therapy to help you through it."

It is a small movement, but Annie notices Oliver draw his brows together as he listens intently.

"You will be able to remember some things," Sharma says, "but there may be other memories you'll never recapture."

"That's okay." Annie smiles. "If it's anything worth remembering, I'll be around to remind him."

"Your sternum is still healing, so your chest will probably be painful for a few more weeks," Sharma continues. "And it will be another six weeks before the cast comes off your leg."

Rahul Sharma is a doctor who prides himself in his bedside manner. He is prudent in his predictions, careful to never offend and cautious about what he discloses, but today he is caught up in the happiness of this family and the pleasure he derives from being part of it. On top of all the warnings and precautions he offers a bit of good news.

"Given enough rehabilitation and rest," he says with a grin, "I think you'll be just fine by time the baby comes along."

Annie gasps. "Baby?"

"Baby?" Oliver croaks.

Annie turns to Oliver. "You spoke! You said baby!"

The corners of Oliver's mouth curl into a stiff smile. "Baby," he repeats.

Annie turns to Sharma. "Are you saying that I'm pregnant?"

"Yes." Sharma nods. His face is beet red. "I apologize. My intention was just to tell you the results of your blood test so it was in my thoughts, but with all the excitement..." He spreads his hands as a simple gesture of regret and says, "I'm afraid I've let the dog out of the sack."

"Cat out of the bag." Annie laughs.

"Ah, yes," Sharma says. "Cat out of the bag."

"How can I not forgive you?" Annie says. "This day is everything I could possibly wish for. You've given me back the love of my life, and now we have another blessing to share."

THAT DAY DOCTOR SHARMA SPENDS nearly two hours with Oliver and Annie, and as a result he is late visiting every one of his patients. It is the first time Rahul has ever been late for anything, and it is also the first time he's ever been spotted walking with such a jaunty step through the hospital corridors.

CELEBRATION TIME

After struggling through all those days of empty silence, Annie is now caught up in a whirlwind of happenings. Within the first few hours Oliver can say words; sentences will come later but for now a single word brings the joy of a song. Every tiny movement is a mountain climbed, a hurdle overcome. Oliver can already move his fingers and wrists but not his arms or legs. Doctor Sharma says in time that will come.

Once they are alone, Annie pulls out her cell phone. "I can't wait to tell Mom and Dad."

As she dials the number at Memory House she tries to think of some clever way to give them this exciting news, but when Ethan Allen answers she blurts out, "Oliver is awake and talking!"

"Is this Annie?" Ethan asks. "I don't think I heard—"

"Yes, it's me, and you heard me correctly; Oliver is awake, and he's able to talk! Not a lot, but that will come in time."

"Thank God," Ethan says. "Laura! Oliver is awake!"

Annie hears the clip, clip, clop of Laura's footsteps as she runs to pick up the extension.

"Is it true?" Laura asks. "Is it honest-to-God true?"

"Yes," Annie answers.

When she hangs up the telephone, she snaps a picture of Oliver with her cell phone. He's not yet smiling, but he's awake and for now that's enough. She attaches it to a quick e-mail and sends it off to Charlie.

Before ten minutes have passed her phone rings.

Charlie's voice is a mixture of joy and disbelief. "Praise the Lord!" he shouts.

"I wanted you to see for yourself," Annie says. "I'll put you on speaker so Oliver can hear you, but he's not up to answering yet."

Charlie's words are short and sweet. "I love you Bro," he says. The happiness in his voice is obvious.

IN LESS THAN AN HOUR ETHAN and Laura are at the hospital. Oliver has the back of his bed cranked up to an angle where he can see visitors, and his eyes are open.

"You are surely a sight for sore eyes," Ethan says. He moves close and gives Oliver a gentle hug. It is a cheek-to-cheek thing, not the manly hug he'd prefer, but Oliver is still frail so for now it is enough. Laura comes from behind him and kisses her son on the cheek.

"You gave us quite a scare," she says. "But all along your daddy knew. He kept telling me, 'Don't worry, Laura, if anybody can beat this thing, it's Oliver.'" As she speaks her hands flutter about him, smoothing the sheet, pushing back a strand of hair fallen across his brow. Even though he is a grown man with a life of his own, she is still his mother and she fusses over him as any mother would.

Oliver tires easily. After a short time his eyes start to droop.

"We should go now," Ethan says.

Laura reluctantly steps away from the bed then stops and looks back.

"We love you, Oliver," she says.

He gives a stiff smile; it is answer enough.

AFTER THEY GO ANNIE ASKS if Oliver would like to rest for a while. He blinks twice.

"That's a yes?" she asks.

He again blinks twice. He has words, but they are heavy and cumbersome to use. As Annie lowers the back of his bed, Oliver says, "Yes, rest." It is the first time he has connected two words.

Annie comes to the side of bed, leans in and kisses his mouth. He moves his fingers to touch her hand.

"Baby," he says and smiles.

Moments later he is asleep.

Annie sits in the chair and watches his chest rise and fall with peaceful easy breaths. The breathing machine is gone from the room, and now there is only the sound of Oliver being alive.

THE EXCITEMENT OF THIS DAY is still pulsing through Annie's veins, so she calls Ophelia to share the good news.

"You were right," she says. "I had to find the right memory to bring Oliver back."

When Ophelia asks what the memory was, Annie tells the story of the book and how it came to her in a dream. "Isn't it odd how one thing can touch so many people's lives and tie us all together?"

"It's not as odd as you might think," Ophelia says. "I believe all of us are connected in some way or another, but only a few people can reach out and find that connection." She hesitates then adds, "You're one of the lucky ones, Annie. It's a gift. Use it wisely, and hang on to it forever."

The weight of Ophelia's words settles in Annie's heart, and

when she promises to do so she knows it is a promise she will forever keep.

THE NEXT PERSON ANNIE CALLS is Max.

"It's nothing short of a miracle," Annie says. "I was reading to Oliver and when I looked up, his eyes were open." She talks of how he is now breathing on his own and capable of speaking.

"This calls for a celebration!" Max says.

"You bet it does," Annie replies. "When Oliver comes home…"

Before she can finish her thought, Annie hears a click; then there is nothing.

"Max?"

No answer.

"Max, are you there?"

Still no answer.

Annie looks at the screen of her phone. It is flashing the low battery signal. "Oh, well," she says and plugs it into the charger.

IT ALMOST NINE-THIRTY WHEN Max tiptoes into Oliver's room. Most of the nurses are gone for the day. Only Phyllis and Liz are on duty.

Max gives a sly grin, then reaches into her tote bag to pull out a bottle of champagne and a stack of plastic party glasses. "Let the celebration begin!"

Annie laughs. "We can't possibly…"

"Sure we can," Max says and pops the cork.

The sound wakes Oliver. Once he is awake, Annie cranks up the back of his bed. This time it is a bit higher than before.

"Max came to visit," she says. "And she brought champagne to celebrate your recovery."

Oliver smiles. "Too soon."

"It's never too soon to celebrate love and friendship," Max says. "You've got to do it while you can. Wait, and someday it might be too late."

"What's that supposed to mean?" Annie asks.

"Just drink," Max answers.

THAT EVENING PHYLLIS, LIZ AND a night porter named Slim all have a glass of champagne. Although Oliver doesn't touch a drop and Annie has only a single sip, this small celebration feels like Mardi Gras.

ANNIE

I can't say whether or not I believed in miracles before, but I surely do now. Oliver waking up as he did had to be a gift from God. There's no other explanation. Even Doctor Sharma admits there's no drug or stimulation device capable of waking a person from a coma. It's up to God and the person. I'd like to think I helped Oliver, but honestly all I did was remind him of the reasons he had for living.

I realize Oliver has a long road ahead of him, but at least we know he's going to make it. Knowing makes everything easier.

For now, Oliver and I are keeping news of the baby to ourselves. It's a secret we want to hold on to for a little while before we share it with the world. Anyway, I want him to be the one to announce it. Seeing Oliver whole and listening to him tell about us having a baby will be more than enough happiness to fill my heart.

I wish I could tell you we created this child on that magical night in the loft, but according to Doctor Sharma it happened a month earlier. He says he did a quantitative blood test, and it indicated I was seven weeks along.

Oliver and I have been married less than five months, but it feels as if we've already lived a lifetime together. It's been tumultuous that's for sure. We never did get to take our honeymoon, and it's probably too late for that now.

I'm thinking maybe we'll just wait, and this time next year we can take a family vacation.

God willing.

OF THINGS TO COME

On Tuesday morning Oliver is transferred to the third floor ambulatory ward. After the silent isolation of the ICU, the hustle and bustle of the third floor is a welcome change. Carts rattle through the hallways, buzzers sound and an endless stream of messages echo across the intercom.

He is not yet able to get out of bed, but Doctor Sharma says it will only be a matter of days. Oliver can already hold a sitting position and shift his right arm forward or backward.

Annie is allowed to stay that first night, but on the second night when the chime that signals the end of visiting hours sounds she is told to leave.

"But I've been with Oliver since the day he was admitted," Annie argues.

Brenda Moss, the night nurse and mother of four teenage boys, is used to arguments and pays them little mind.

"That's the rule," she says flatly.

"Oliver needs me. If—"

"Not anymore," Brenda cuts in. "He doesn't need you anymore. He's doing fine, better than most."

A washboard of doubt settles on Annie's forehead. "I'd feel better if—"

"You'd feel better if you got a good night's sleep and let my patient do the same," Brenda says. "So scoot. I promise to take good care of your husband."

Annie is left with no alternative. Before she leaves, she places her cell phone in Oliver's lap where it is within easy reach.

"The house is on speed dial," she says. "If you need anything, anything at all, just press one and I'll come back."

"I. Am. Fine," he answers. In a single day Oliver has begun to hook words together. He can now express his thoughts; however, putting the words together is a slow and tiring process.

"I know you're fine." Annie says. "But I wanted you to realize that I'm available if you need me." She tries to make this reply sound nonchalant, but behind her words is a gigantic ball of fear.

IT IS NEAR TEN WHEN Annie arrives at Memory House. The house is dark. Ethan and Laura are already asleep. Now that Oliver is doing well, they are thinking about returning home to Florida. In a few days they will be gone.

Guided by the glow of the hall nightlight, Annie climbs the stairs. In the loft there is only the light of the moon and stars. It is enough.

Wearing a clean tee shirt and panties, she slides under the comforter. The bed still has the smell of Oliver's aftershave. So much has changed and yet...

She looks up at the stars, and it is as if Oliver is there beside her. She hears the sound of his laughter and then her own voice.

I wonder if we've made a baby tonight...

Annie bolts upright. She knows she has found the memory

they've left in this room. The sweetness of it is almost overwhelming. Throughout the long hours of the night, she thinks back on all of the memories she and Oliver have made and she comes to realize the sweetest of all is yet to come.

Moments before the sun crosses the horizon she cradles an arm around her tummy.

"Come on, little one," she says, "it's time for us to get some sleep. Tomorrow we'll go visit your daddy."

Annie slips beneath the comforter and closes her eyes. This night she doesn't dream about the past; she dreams of the future. She sees herself with crinkles at the corners of her eyes and grandchildren on her knee. Oliver sits beside her. His hair is silver, and he looks remarkably like his father.

"Remember when..." he whispers in her ear, and they both laugh.

The sun is high in the sky when Annie wakes. The dream is gone, but so are her fears. She has seen tomorrow, and it is truly beautiful.

A TIME OF RENEWAL

Oliver is at the hospital for more than a month. Nine days after he is moved to the third floor, he has the second surgery on his leg. This time Annie does not sit and weep. She has begun crocheting baby blankets, so she sits alongside Max in the waiting room and adds another nine rows of stitching to the yellow blanket.

THE BABY IS NO LONGER a secret. The day Ethan and Laura came to the hospital to say goodbye, Oliver told them. It wasn't the elegant speech they'd planned; he simply patted Annie's tummy and said, "Our baby."

Laura already had her suspicions. She'd seen the look in Annie's eyes. It's a look every mother recognizes, one of pure unadulterated happiness.

ONCE OLIVER'S PARENTS KNOW, ANNIE can't wait to tell Ophelia, Max and Giselle. She calls them all three that same afternoon.

"With a baby and the apothecary, it looks like I may not be coming back to work for quite a while," she tells Giselle.

"I suspected as much," Giselle replies. "The night of the party I thought…"

Giselle says she's already hired a trainee who she admits doesn't have Annie's perceptive abilities but should work out well.

Max is the next call. She claims she had no idea.

"Was it that night you launched the loft?" she jokes.

Annie laughs along with her. "According to the doctor it was a month earlier."

They chat for a while, but before they hang up Annie tells Max she might want to start thinking about what it means to be a godmother. That afternoon Max sets aside the insurance office layout she's working on and starts designing a baby's room.

The final call is to Ophelia. Annie has saved this call for last because it is the most special. When she shares the news, Annie says, "I'd like to think you'll be a grandmother to the baby and teach him or her to appreciate the magic of life as you did me."

"Her," Ophelia replies. "Your baby's a girl. A girl who's going to have the same abilities you have."

"How in the world can you know that?" Annie asks.

Ophelia laughs. "Magic."

What Ophelia has forecasted is only a premonition. A wish, perhaps. Only time will tell if she is right, but Annie somehow thinks she is.

ACCORDING TO DOCTOR SHARMA, OLIVER'S rehabilitation is progressing beautifully. In just three short weeks he has gone from struggling to lift an arm to a full-blown strength-building program in the rehabilitation center.

Walter is the therapist assigned to Oliver. He is a man with a strange sense of humor and shoulders that fill the doorway. For the first few days, he comes to the room and eases Oliver into the simple stretching range of motion exercises.

Lifting Oliver's palm against his, he says, "Hokay, now push my hand back."

Since Walter is as solid as a cement wall such a feat is impossible, but Oliver tries. After two minutes of pushing, Walter relaxes his hand and lets Oliver succeed.

"Gut job," Walter says. "Gut job. Now ve do de udder hand."

OLIVER HAS MOVED ON TO standing and walking. The cast on his leg is cumbersome and heavy, but he now has enough upper body strength to balance himself on the walker and thump his way down the hallway to the sunroom.

Twice a day Oliver spends ninety minutes in the rehabilitation room; the rest of the day he is free to do as he pleases. Annie comes to visit every day. Max stops by in the evening.

Ophelia and Lillian come on Monday, Wednesday and Friday at 3PM. It is a schedule they have set up with the Baylor automobile services. They bring their pinochle cards and play at the table in the sunroom. Oliver has come to love the game as they do and claims this is something they should continue even after he has left the hospital. On occasion Annie joins the game, but now that she has started crocheting a pink sweater she has less of an interest in cards.

DURING THE WEEKS OLIVER IS in the hospital he and Annie spend many long hours talking. Sometimes they speak of the future, and sometimes they talk about all that has happened. Annie tells him of the days when he was in a coma and Doctor Sharma's many kindnesses.

"Were you aware of any of that?" she asks.

Oliver says there are things he can remember: the sound of her voice, the touch of her hand on his. He cannot point to a word or a specific instance; all of those memories are shadows seen in a darkened room. He remembers the smell of coffee and the saltiness of tears. Sometimes at night when the third floor has gone quiet and most patients are asleep, he can close his eyes and still feel the weight of her head against her shoulder. He knows this is one thing he will never forget.

Although the cast is still on his right leg and will be there for another two weeks, Oliver is scheduled to come home the Friday before Thanksgiving. It will be another six weeks before he can return to work, but already he is planning to have the clerk bring a few case files to the house so he can prepare himself. He misses being at the courthouse just as Annie has missed working in the apothecary.

OLIVER

Day after tomorrow I go home. It seems somehow strange to be saying that. With so many pieces of my memory missing it's as if I'm starting a new life. Annie is my one constant. She is my bridge between what is and what was.

I remember most of my life, but there's a section missing. A month, maybe two months before the accident is gone. Not really gone I suppose, just misplaced. It's somewhere in my brain, and Doctor Sharma believes little by little I'll be able to find it.

Annie told me about us moving into the loft. She says we were lying in bed, looking up at the stars and planning our life together, and when she talks about it her eyes glisten. I know this is a special memory, and it saddens me to say I don't remember. I thought Annie would be upset by not my remembering, but she wasn't. She gave me this funny little smile and said in that case we'd just have to do it all over again.

The accident is also gone, but not remembering that is somewhat of a blessing. I don't remember being in an ambulance or coming to the hospital, but I remember Annie being in the room with me. Not her face, but the sound of her voice and the feel of her hands touching me. It was as if my eyes had been taken away but my other senses were left in place.

This accident has changed our lives, mine and Annie's both. I guess almost dying makes you realize how lucky you are to be living.

People often talk about having a guardian angel. I'm luckier than most. I married mine.

The Homecoming

The sun is brilliant, but there is a chill in the air on the Friday Oliver comes home from the hospital. Annie has prayed there will be no rain this day, and she has gotten her wish.

After she has packed the things accumulated during his stay at Mercy General, an orderly comes with a wheelchair. When they start down the hallway, she runs ahead to bring the car around.

Oliver is waiting when Annie pulls up to the front door. He smiles as he lifts himself from the wheelchair to a standing position. He leans heavily on the cane, but he can move on his own and prefers to do so. He now has a walking cast on his right leg. It will come off next week, but Doctor Sharma warns there is to be no driving for at least two weeks.

Annie gets out, comes around and opens the passenger door. She has pushed the front seat back as far as it will go to accommodate the bulky cast. Climbing into the car is a slow process, but Oliver manages. Annie's fingers itch to lift his leg for him, buckle his seat belt, adjust the position of his foot, but she holds back. These are things he wants to do for himself. He is forging a pathway back to normalcy, and too much help will only slow his progress.

A number of friends and neighbors have mentioned coming to visit, but Annie has asked them to wait until next week. She wants to spend a few days alone with Oliver. It is a time to reconnect and remember.

She is hopeful the magic of Memory House will bring back some of what Oliver has lost. Unfortunately it is now too cool to lie on a blanket beneath the stars, and the loft will have to wait until he is strong enough to climb the stairs. But there are other familiar touchstones, and she is counting on those.

When he first steps inside the door, Oliver gives a nostalgic sigh. The living room is familiar. The sofa, chairs, bookcases are all part of the memories he still has.

"Do you remember the new study?" Annie asks.

A puzzled look settles on Oliver's face. He is uncertain.

She leads him down the hallway, walking slowly enough for him to keep pace but not offering assistance.

"I've hung your painting of the Wyattsville courthouse in here," Annie says. At the doorway she steps back so he is the first to enter.

He steps inside the room and looks across at the desk. The mug filled with pens and pencils, the clock, the notebook left open—everything is as it should be. He turns to Annie and smiles.

"I remember this room," he says.

He goes to the desk and lifts the notebook. *Ella Mae Grimley* he has written. There are notes on both the boy and girl. *Margaret Grimley, angry and vindictive,* the notes say.

Oliver stands there for a moment, and he can picture Ella Mae, a thin girl, barely old enough to be called a woman. Two children clinging to her skirt and an angry mother-in-law scowling across the courtroom.

He looks at the date on the notes. October 12. The weekend before the accident, yet he remembers.

For now that's how Oliver's memory file is arranged. This happened before the accident; that happened after. It is a dividing line of time. It won't always be this way. In the years to come that line will become blurred or change altogether. Oliver knows life is filled with the events by which we measure time. Perhaps next year or the year after he will say, "Oh, that happened the year the baby was born" and "This was the summer we planted the oak tree."

ROOM BY ROOM THEY WALK through the house. Some things Oliver remembers; others are only vaguely familiar.

In the early afternoon Annie brews a pot of dandelion tea and fixes a plate of sandwiches. "Would you like to have lunch on the back porch?" she asks.

Oliver nods.

The air is cool, but the sun warms their shoulders. Annie has a cozy covering the pot, and when she pours the tea a small puff of steam rises from the cup. Oliver sips it slowly.

"It's very peaceful out here," he says.

"It's my second favorite spot in the house," Annie replies.

Oliver smiles. "Your favorite is the loft, right?"

Annie returns his smile and nods.

After lunch Oliver moves to the recliner in the living room and dozes. He tires easily, and Doctor Sharma has warned that he will need plenty of rest. Annie has already put a down comforter on the bed in the small downstairs room. When Oliver is stronger they will return to the loft, but for now she will be happy just to feel the warmth of his body lying beside hers.

While Oliver naps, Annie starts preparing dinner. Tonight is a homecoming so she is making his favorite: lamb stew. On the sideboard there is a bottle of Pinot Noir she has saved for this occasion.

While the thick slices of bacon are sizzling in the iron skillet, she rolls the chunks of lamb in a mix of flour and finely-ground eyebright. It is an herb that will help shed light on shadowy memories.

Annie adds the crumbled bacon, carrots, potatoes and onion to the pot, then turns to the counter and rolls out a round of biscuit dough. Just as she is about to pop them into the oven, Oliver appears at the door.

"Is that lamb stew I smell?"

Annie turns with a smile. "It certainly is. A welcome home dinner to show how much I've missed having you here."

"I've missed being here," he replies.

He crosses the room, leans down and kisses the top of Annie's shoulder. "This seems like a dinner we should be having on the back porch."

Annie is unsure if this suggestion is brought about by a memory or just a spur of the moment thought. "It's going to be pretty chilly outside once the sun goes down."

He grins. "We can wear sweaters."

She sees the gleam in his eye and knows this is a memory.

THAT EVENING ANNIE MOVES A small heater to the porch, and they bundle themselves in wool sweaters. She sets out a cluster of five candles just as she did that Friday before the accident, and they have dinner at the small table.

It is too chilly to linger afterward, so they come inside.

As she washes the dishes and sets them into the drainer, she hears the thump, thump, thump of Oliver's cane moving through the house. She is just finishing up when she hears him call her name.

Annie wipes her hands and hurries to the living room, but he is not there. She checks the bedroom and then the hall bath.

"Where are you?" she finally calls out.

"Come to the hall," he answers.

She does and when Annie looks up, Oliver is halfway up the staircase.

He looks down and grins. "Let's go find that memory I've misplaced."

IN THE WEEKS THAT FOLLOW, Annie reopens the apothecary and Oliver settles at the desk in his study. Every other day the clerk from his office comes with a new package of files for Oliver to review. They work together for an hour or two, then the clerk returns with a list of assignments: research this case, find a precedent for such-and-such a ruling, bring back a report on any priors.

Before the month is out Oliver has few, if any, holes in his memory.

IN JANUARY ON A FRIDAY evening when Oliver sits in his study browsing through the *Richmond Times-Dispatch* he happens across a small article on page 6 of the Regional News Section.

DRUNK DRIVER GETS 2 YEARS

January 29, 2015, Second District Court of Virginia: Danny Logan, a multiple offender, was sentenced to two years in the Coffeewood Correctional Center for a third DUI offense. At the time of the accident Logan was driving without a valid license. His license had been suspended for a previous DUI offense in September of 2014.

Logan pled No Contest to the charge.

Samuel Harkins, the presiding judge, said, "This incident was so horrendous it is a miracle the victim survived. Had he not, this would have been a manslaughter charge, and Logan would be looking at 20 years to life."

Although there is a photo of accident aftermath, there is no mention of Oliver's name.

When Oliver looks at the photo, he remembers the accident. It plays like a slow motion movie running through his mind. He remembers the phone flying from his hand. He can picture the split second the truck slammed into the side of his car, the explosion of the airbag, the policeman at the window, the fireman lifting his leg free. He can hear the sound of sirens growing closer, and then there is nothing.

Nothing until Annie's shadow speaks to him.

Oliver folds the newspaper and slides it into the bottom of his briefcase. On Monday he will return to work at the courthouse, and he will dispose of the newspaper there. This is the one memory he will forever keep from Annie.

THE SCALE OF LIFE

When the Keeper of the Scale watches Oliver Doyle climb the staircase toward the loft, he gives a huge sigh of relief. On the earth it is felt as a gust of wind. A swirl of red and gold leaves tumble from the oaks surrounding the Good Shepherd Church, and the branches of the willow at Memory House sway.

For the moment, Annie Doyle's scale is in balance.

The Keeper knows this will be short-lived. A baby is on the way. Before the year is out, Annie's scale will again be weighted on the happiness side.

She is one of those rare individuals capable of happiness so great it spills over into other lives. In the time she has known Ophelia Browne, she has caused Ophelia's scale to weigh heavily on the happiness side. And were it not for the accident, Oliver's scale would have bottomed out with what is known as overwhelming joy.

Max Martinelli, Annie's friend, is a girl who, with the exception of that one year in Paris, has always been perfectly level. But as he gazes into the future, the Keeper can see Max's scale will soon be totally out of balance. It will happen because of what Annie tells her.

He wearily shakes his head. The Keeper knows this will come to pass, but he has no power to ordain the events of life; his job is simply to maintain the balance of sorrow and happiness.

TONIGHT ANNIE WILL LOOK UP and see the stars in the night sky. The scale is there between Spica and Antares, but she will not see it again until next summer.

Even then—even when the scale is visible in the sky—no mortal can see the balance of their scale. This only the Keeper sees.

Since the start of time he has carried the weight of this responsibility, so he stands ready with a collection of small round river rocks made smooth by years of wear and worry. When the time is right, he will balance each mortal's scale, just as he has done for all these many centuries.

From the Author

THE LOFT IS BOOK TWO IN THE MEMORY HOUSE SERIES. I hope it has settled in your heart as it has in mine.

I would love to hear what you enjoyed and what you didn't. I'd like to know what you'd like more of, and if you have a story to share I am always ready to listen. The best stories are usually the ones that start with a grain of truth and then grow into something magical.

You can contact me through my blog at betteleecrosby.com, and while you are there sign up for my newsletter. It's a fun way to stay in touch and every month there's a special giveaway for all of the friends and fans who open the newsletter e-mail to see what's new.

I look forward to seeing you there.

~ *Bette Lee Crosby*

Turn the page for more heartwarming stories.

MEMORY HOUSE
The Memory House Series, Book One

Annie Cross is running from a broken love affair when she stops at the Memory House Bed and Breakfast Inn. She is looking to forget the past, but what she finds is a future filled with the magic of memories left behind by others. A heartwarming story of love and friendship. Winner of a FAPA President's Book Award Medal.

SPARE CHANGE
The Wyattsville Series, Book One

Winner of five Literary Awards, Spare Change has been compared to John Grisham's The Client. Eleven year-old Ethan Allen Doyle has witnessed a brutal murder and now the boy is running for his life. Olivia Westerly is the only person he can trust, and he's not too sure he can trust her. She's got no love of children and a truckload of superstitions—one of them is the belief that eleven is the unluckiest number on earth.

JUBILEE'S JOURNEY
The Wyattsville Series, Book Two

Winner of the 2014 FPA President's Book Award Gold Medal, Jubilee's Journey is the story of a child born in the West Virginia mountains and orphaned before she is seven. When she and her older brother go in search of an aunt, he is caught up in a crime not of his making. Jubilee knows the truth, but who is going to believe a seven-year-old child?

PASSING THROUGH PERFECT
The Wyattsville Series, Book Three

Passing through Perfect is a story rife with the injustices of the South and rich with the compassion of strangers. It's 1946. The war is over. Millions of American soldiers are coming home and Benjamin Church is one of them. After four years of being away he thought things in Alabama would have changed, but they haven't. Grinder's Corner is as it's always been — a hardscrabble burp in the road. It's not much, but it's home.

THE TWELFTH CHILD
The Serendipity Series, Book One

The Twelfth Child is an uplifting tale of trust, love and friendship. To escape a planned marriage, a willful daughter leaves home and makes her way in a Depression-era world. When she is nearing the tail end of her years, she meets the young woman with whom she forges a friendship that lasts beyond life.

PREVIOUSLY LOVED TREASURES
The Serendipity Series, Book Two

Previously Loved Treasures is a story that resonates with heartwarming albeit quirky characters and the joy of a pay-it-forward philosophy. When Ida Sweetwater opens a rooming house, she will find the granddaughter she never knew she had and turn a group of haphazard strangers into a family.

WISHING FOR WONDERFUL
The Serendipity Series, Book Three

Wishing for Wonderful is a story narrated by a Cupid with attitude. It will have you laughing out loud as Cupid uses a homeless dog in his scheme to give two deserving couples the love they deserve.

WHAT MATTERS MOST

In What Matters Most Louise Palmer is faced with life-altering changes and must choose between friendships and marriage. Although it is at times laugh-out-loud funny, beneath the humor there is a message of love, tolerance and coming to grips with reality.

CRACKS IN THE SIDEWALK

A *USA Today* Bestseller and Winner of the 2014 Reader's Favorite Gold Medal, Cracks in the Sidewalk is a powerful family saga that is a heartrending reminder of how fragile relationships can be. Based on the true story of a woman's search for her missing grandchildren.

BLUEBERRY HILL

Blueberry Hill asks the poignant question—can love save a person from self-destruction? In a heartrending memoir Crosby looks back to a time when the sisters were young enough to feel invincible and foolish enough to believe it would last forever.

ABOUT THE AUTHOR

AWARD-WINNING NOVELIST BETTE LEE CROSBY brings the wit and wisdom of her Southern Mama to works of fiction—the result is a delightful blend of humor, mystery and romance.

"Storytelling is in my blood," Crosby laughingly admits, "My mom was not a writer, but she was a captivating storyteller, so I find myself using bits and pieces of her voice in most everything I write."

Crosby's work was first recognized in 2006 when she received The National League of American Pen Women Award for a then unpublished manuscript. Since then, she has gone on to win numerous other awards, including The Reviewer's Choice Award, FPA President's Book Award Gold Medal and The Royal Palm Literary Award.

To learn more about Bette Lee Crosby, explore her other work, or read a sample from any of her books, visit her blog at:

http://betteleecrosby.com

Made in the USA
Lexington, KY
30 November 2015